# A CLOSET FEMINIST

# A CLOSET FEMINIST

## A NOVEL BY

## CARLA SARETT

For information contact:
Unsolicited Press
Portland, Oregon
www.unsolicitedpress.com
orders@unsolicitedpress.com
619-354-8005

Cover Design: Kathryn Gerhardt
Editor: Jay Kristensen Jr.

ISBN: 978-1-956692-02-0

# CONTENTS

I thank Judith Orlowski for her good-humored guidance and support. Portions of this novel appeared in the stories "Career Girl" in *Love Hurts* (Eric's Hysterics, 2013) and "Skinny Girl" in *Red Fez* (Issue 46)

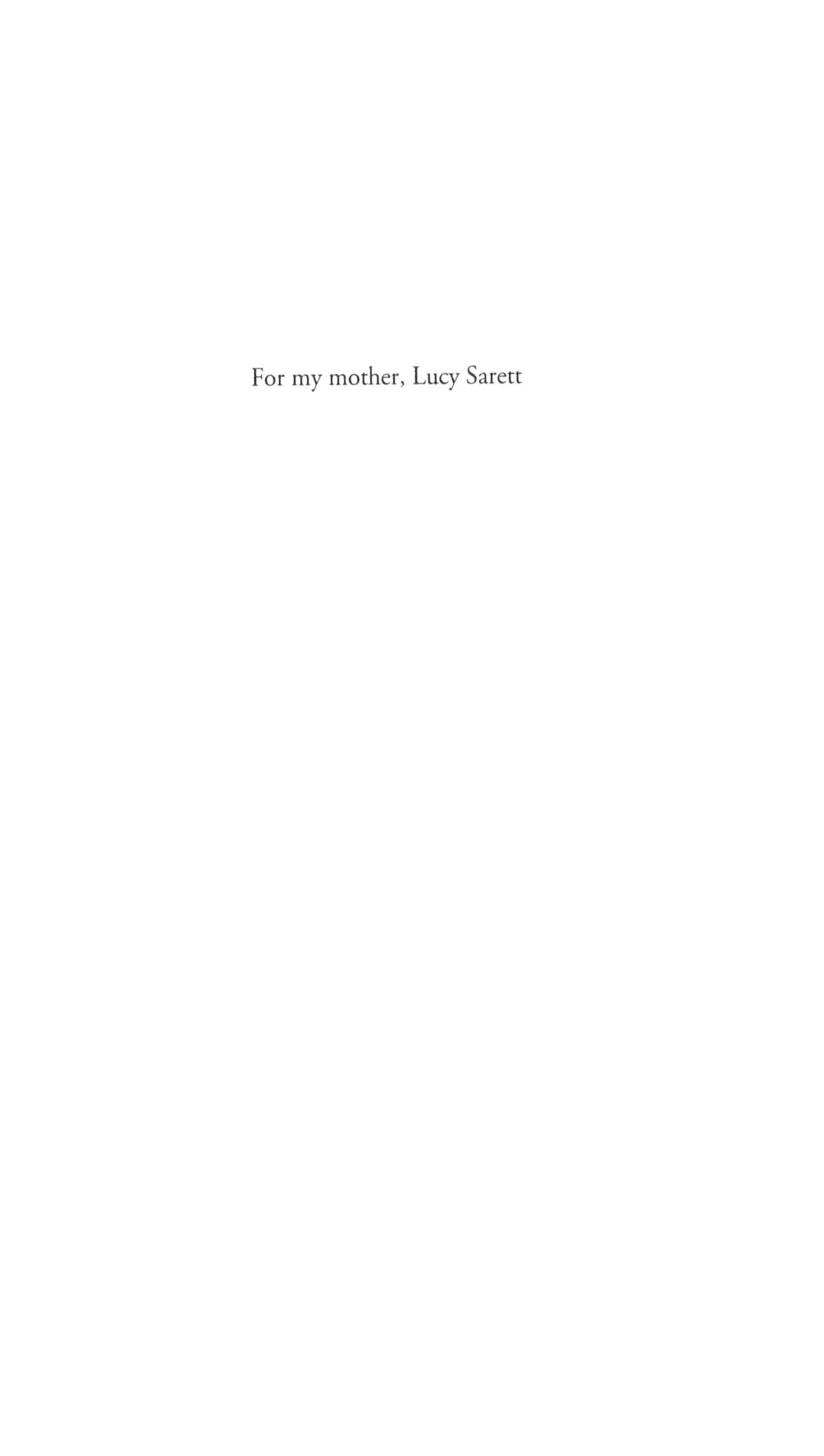

For my mother, Lucy Sarett

# ONE

Breathe in, breathe out, I told myself, hoping against hope to achieve that inner peace everyone spoke about. I closed my eyes in search of a blurb for *Aunt Zelda's Flying Umbrella*. "Letitia Worth has written another delight, filled with the elusive mysteries of childhood," I wrote—a phrase recycled time and time again, only with different authors. It was fitting, in a way. Since I never bothered to read any of the books in question, their contents would remain, permanently, a mystery to me as well. And I waited for the clock to strike noon.

I was meeting a man for lunch—a certain Peter Greene. He was attractive in a New York intellectual way, speaking in flowing sentences, like one of those surprisingly clever men in French movies. His passions were Marxism, politics, and high-quality audio equipment, perhaps in the reverse order, though.

After the lecture at the New School on the origins of anti-Semitism we had hopped on the same uptown bus, and ended up at a neighborhood bar with sawdust on the floor. In one of those New York moments, I learned that he was my boss's younger brother. By another coincidence, Peter's apartment was only three blocks from mine, on East 80th, in one of those sunless East Side apartments with brick walls and hardwood floors. There was no way to make such dim places cozy, and Peter hadn't tried— everything looked brand new, untouched. We sat and listened to Sinatra. There was some discussion about the difference between cold digital sound, and the other warm sound—was it vacuum?

Grateful that I did not have to endure an evening of Led Zeppelin, I said, "It does sound warm."

And here we were, the day after, at a Greek coffee shop around the corner from my office. In hindsight, an unromantic choice; the neighborhood was fairly seedy.

Peter's meal-ordering process was complex and time-consuming. He vacillated between sandwiches and salads. He probed the tired waiter about his culinary options. Eventually, he settled, nervously, on a grilled Swiss and fries, or #15 in coffee-shop lingo. I was relieved to have that part of our meal over.

Still, it was a treat to have lunch with a real companion, and not sit alone at the counter. I felt Peter Greene and I had much in common in the books and ideas department. I envisioned us debating Marxist theory over a glass of chilled white wine, or attending a museum lecture—that sort of thing.

He leaned toward me and said, "Bella, you're not my type, but I'm really into you."

"Your type," I repeated. "I'm not?"

"No, not really," he said, wiping his wire-rimmed glasses.

Instinct told me when men, especially men like Peter, had a type, the girls in question were tall and blonde, and wore cashmere and pearls. I instantly reviewed all of the types I was not: not tall, not short, not blonde, not redheaded, not almond-eyed, not to mention perky or cute. To be sure, it was a long list.

I contemplated my newly discovered identity as a medium-height, medium-weight brunette with no defining features. Looking around, I saw more than a few twenty-something New York brunettes who could have doubled for me in a pinch. Although now that I bothered to look, they were better dressed and thinner than I was.

These unwelcome insights made me glum. "I guess you're not my type either," I confessed.

"What do you mean, I'm not your type? What's your type?" he snapped.

I considered his question as the waiter placed plates on the table. My college boyfriends had nothing in common, apart from the obvious fact that they ended up as ex-boyfriends. But being an ex-boyfriend hardly made them a type, or at least I hoped not, since one of them seemed downright psychotic.

"Hmm, maybe the kind of man who doesn't have a type. I think that's my type."

"That's the problem with feminism. Here I am, trying to give you a compliment, and you're twisting my words," Peter said, in true debating-team style.

"Well, that's the problem. I mean, a compliment is, 'You're wonderful,'" I pointed out. "A compliment is, 'You look nice in that sweater.' That's a real compliment. Anyway, I'm not a feminist, whatever you think a feminist is."

I delicately plucked a single French fry from his plate, as if to prove the point.

He pounced on my logic. "What do you mean you're not a feminist? You're just being facile. That is what women always do to evade the issue."

"You see, it's all about work. I think most feminists like to work and I hate work," I said. "Some women like it, which is fine. But I wish I could just hang out or see lots of movies. Maybe I would work just one day a week, you know, for fun, like in a museum, or maybe not, maybe just read a lot of novels. You know what I mean?"

My rambling had grated on Peter. "That's not the point. The point is, you, you're taking it personally like I was insulting you. So, you're not Marilyn Monroe. I came downtown to tell you what a great night I had."

I returned to my Greek salad, more sanguine than before. No girl could be Marilyn Monroe, after all—and it tickled me that Peter had resurrected her in the era of free love.

"Not that I want to marry you," he continued, drowning his French fries in a pool of ketchup. "Don't get the wrong idea."

The coffee shop had turned noisy with so many waiters shouting— "Number fifteen! Fourteen! Whiskey dry!"—so, it was hard to make myself heard. "My guess is this coffee shop's filled with men who don't want to marry me. Come to think of it, all of Manhattan's filled with men who don't want to marry me."

I boomed so loudly that an older woman eyed me with alarm. She probably thought I was a hardened floozy.

"So now what? You're angry because I'm not proposing? I'm not crazy or something where I'm going to ask a girl I hardly know to marry me. You don't expect that, do you?"

"Calm down, I don't want to marry you," I said. I meant to emphasize the "marry" part like an ardent feminist, which I was not, but who cared? Instead, I ended up broadcasting the "you" part like an outraged lover.

I was sorry for my shrill tone. I had no license to tell Peter Greene that sex without love is just sex, even if you play music in the background, even if you think it's great sex, it's still just sex; and men and women either move closer or further apart; there's no standing still. Who was I to tell anyone anything?

Peter jumped in before I could apologize. "So you don't want to." He now acted as if he had proposed on bended knees, and I had cruelly rejected him.

"No, I do not," I answered. "We're just having lunch. That's all. We're not talking about marriage. Actually, we don't even have a relationship, not a real relationship. Nothing's happening here, nothing."

And it was just then that I noticed dark-eyed Jeremy Levy, who worked two floors above me—I had spent months trying to catch his attention. He was ordering a sandwich, and he heard me turning Peter down, or so he thought. And this time, Jeremy looked at me and smiled, the barest hint of a smile, but it was enough for me.

Peter said, "So you're into someone else?"

I shrugged helplessly.

"Unbelievable," Peter said, "you are un-be-lievable. My sister said you were crazy, like maybe on drugs, always tripping into things and coming in late, and making excuses for yourself. She said you had problems and you have all these headaches, and you're always talking about the Holocaust. She said you might be crazy."

That was news, although it should not have been. I had hardly proved a model employee. Rita had hidden her disdain well, though. She had been polite. That much, I had to grant her.

I said, "I didn't know—about Rita, I mean." I knew the part about myself all too well. I knew that part better than anyone.

Peter said, "Yeah, she wants to fire you, but she can't think of a reason. She's had a hard year and she really needs someone she can count on."

"A hard year," I repeated, mostly to myself.

Peter did not walk me back, which was just as well. I felt trapped between an apology and a complaint, without much feeling behind either. Besides, who knew what he might repeat to Rita, who had cast me as a lunatic—and a lazy lunatic, too.

After lunch, I marched into Rita's office. As usual, she was wearing a fabulous designer suit and bold, colored earrings. "So you don't like me, and you think I'm crazy," I said, not repeating the lazy part, since that was true.

She finished licking an envelope. "I do like you. I just told Peter that you're doing a lousy job. You're smart—there's no reason you couldn't do a better job. But I get it, the work's boring and the pay's not good. But, Bella, these writers depend on us."

I made a lame gesture of apology. "I'll try, really, I will."

Rita calmly licked another envelope and said, "Maybe you will, maybe you won't. Anyway, it seems you spend all your time chasing Jeremy Levy. But I guess he doesn't mind."

"He doesn't?" I asked, forgetting all about the job and Peter, and even Rita.

"Not from what I can tell," she said, opening another file.

Minutes later, I was standing in Jeremy's doorway. For a moment, I almost lost my nerve—I saw a tennis racket, and I was hopelessly un-athletic. Maybe Jeremy needed a doubles partner for a girlfriend. But I forged ahead.

"Do you have a type?" I asked—I could not say his name, it felt too soon.

He weighed my question like a riddle. He pretended to scribble a few notes, and I moved close behind him so he could smell my perfume. Then he stopped his scribbling and we faced one another. We were only inches apart. His dark eyes looked less restless than usual, less distracted.

"Women. Women are my type," he said. And then he smiled at me, just as he had earlier in the coffee shop.

"So, I could be your type," I said, "I mean, with such broad parameters."

# TWO

"I need to go on a diet," I told my mother over the phone. "I can tell from the way waitresses look at me. In New York, all the waitresses are super-skinny, which is counter-intuitive if you think about it."

"Some women never gain weight even when they eat all the time—it's most peculiar. But I've heard that the grapefruit diet works, and Selma Fine says that she lived on only hot dogs for a few weeks and she lost over twenty pounds," said my mother, who was forever gaining and losing the same twenty. "But don't lose too much—Jeremy Levy likes you the way you are."

"He'll like me better after the hot dog or the grapefruit diet."

"Just the hot dogs, not the buns," advised my mother sagely. "If you eat the buns, it doesn't work."

"Probably something to do with metabolism," I concluded.

At the supermarket counter, I found a pocket-sized book called *The Top 100 Diets that Really Work for You!* The top diets included the hamburger diet, the hot dog diet, the bread-only diet, the rice diet, the apple cider diet, as well as the famed "celebrity" grapefruit diet, which required eating grapefruit before meals of Melba toast and low-fat cottage cheese, and then extra grapefruit slices in between. There was even a Fig Newton diet—which, amazingly, I tried, and which destroyed my taste for that particular cookie once and for all. In the end, though, I settled upon the "eating less" diet. Perhaps if I'd published this secret technique, I might have made a small fortune—it turned out to be foolproof and required no special skills.

As I was shrinking, work took a downhill turn. My job in the children's book department was deemed "redundant" and I was laid off with two weeks' severance. But even so, I saw a silver lining. It could be worse, I told myself. I could have gained weight—and then a job would not matter at all, according to my murky reasoning.

The company's farewell party for the laid-off victims was held in the copying room, of all places. Everyone squeezed between grey file cabinets and Xerox machines, on which there were sad paper plates, jug wine, and boxes of Ritz crackers. I hadn't bothered to learn anyone's name. Under the circumstances, I felt it high time for a drink.

Jeremy arrived late, at which point I was on my third glass of cheap wine. "Here," he said, offering me a Ritz cracker.

I brushed away the enemy cracker. "I need to lose weight," I informed him loftily. The cracker, for all I knew, might be half the calories of a glass of white wine.

"Why?" he asked, confused.

"Because," I said.

By then the mid-afternoon wine hit me, and the fluorescent light hurt my eyes. I wobbled, unsupported by my black skinny stilettos. Jeremy, who wore penny loafers and shirts with little alligators on them, looked down. "Can you walk in those?"

"As a matter of fact, I bought these shoes in London. Most men find them very sexy." A few women perked up at my loud mention of hordes of stiletto-loving men.

Jeremy separated me from my drink. "That's great," he muttered.

He quickly pulled me past the grey file cabinets and plastic cups and I followed, tottering on my 4-inch heels. In the elevator, I leaned against him and announced, "I am not really that drunk."

He did not look happy. "You're drunk enough, Bella."

"You know what I mean. And, we don't have to walk, anyway," I said.

"I know what you mean," he said. His lips formed a no, and I sulked.

On Madison, he hailed a taxi and paid the driver in advance and then he gave me a depressingly chaste kiss, as if we had never kissed. I gave Jeremy one last sort of sultry look, which he pretended not to notice. I slammed the door before he could shut it for me.

I slumped in the backseat and heard the driver say, in a foreign accent, "He is a nice guy—clean cut."

"He doesn't drink and he doesn't do drugs. He drinks milk," I told the driver who, I saw, wore an enormous turban. Maybe he was a Sikh and carried a silver sword, although I felt it best not to inquire about that.

"This is very healthy," he said. "Drugs, these are bad things— you should not do them." His fierce warrior eyes met mine in his rearview mirror.

"And wine always gives me a migraine," I said.

"Milk, this is healthy," the turban-wearer replied triumphantly.

I must have flubbed interviews at every trade publisher, health publisher, Jewish publisher, scholarly journal, and, naturally, all of the "girl" magazines—*Seventeen, Cosmopolitan, Glamour*. I was probed about heady intellectual matters like wordplay in *Finnegan's Wake*, after which a kindly grey-haired woman would add as a polite afterthought, "Now there is *some* typing involved." Afterward, she would look dismayed. "Let's see. You got sixty words a minute, but you made, oh, thirty mistakes. But keep trying!" My typing skills over time worsened, which was mystifying.

But eventually, I stumbled upon a low-level position as a copyeditor for a technical publisher. The office was quiet—rows of wholesome-looking men in ties and white shirts with, in those days, slide rules, metrics and scales, and thick volumes with titles like *Principles of Heating*. On the whole, its orderliness appealed to me.

My future boss was a tall stout man with a small red face and a jolly manner, which I would have hated to disturb. "It's not the most interesting work," Mr. Peterson assured me with the voice of one who had once dreamed of greater things but who took his present position in stride. "A young woman like you might find it boring."

"I doubt that, Mr. Peterson," I said, since I was wearing my new navy suit and pumps. "Besides, I like scientists."

He shook his head, sadly. "We are not true scientists, but we do contribute to science, in our way."

"Definitely, Mr. Peterson," I agreed. "Manuals need to be clear, don't they?"

"You'll probably be off to graduate school in a few years," he said without complaint. "My daughter is getting her master's in criminal sociology at Columbia. Are you interested in the field of sociology?"

"A little," I said, not wanting to offend his clever daughter's choice. "Maybe not for a career, though."

"My other daughter's getting married," he said, with a more satisfied tone. "I suppose you're interested in marriage."

"That depends on the groom, Mr. Peterson," I replied.

I was hired on the spot.

My work focused on the switch to the "new style," in which hyphens were banished for reasons unknown. I pictured a Style Dictator exiling the unloved hyphens and dashes. "It's sad to see 'hydro-electric' turn into 'hydroelectric.' I love these hyphens," I lamented to my partner in copyediting, Sue Olinsky. "To me, 'fare-well' is poignant and 'farewell' is mundane."

"We wouldn't have jobs if it weren't for the hyphens," said Sue. "It's progress. Things change. No reason to have hyphens in compound words."

Sue Olinsky was a no-nonsense person. She spoke of dry cleaning, ironing boards, checking accounts, pantyhose, vacuum cleaners, and food prices at different supermarkets. There was a universe of practical information that people like Sue apparently knew about.

"I didn't know eggs cost more at some places than at others," I said. "That is very useful to know, I mean, when I make an omelet."

She threw up her large hands. "How doesn't someone know that?"

I doubted that my mother knew the cost of eggs at different markets or the cost of much of anything. "I don't buy food much," I said, dazzled by the plentitude of facts at Sue's disposal.

"No kidding," she said.

"I'm kind of not hungry," I said, meaning I had not heard from Jeremy in months.

Sometimes, Sue urged me to take matters into my own hands and call him. "He didn't reject you. He was being noble," Sue argued. "That's a guy thing, not taking advantage of a girl when she's drunk or stoned. It's kind of sweet in a stupid way."

"I'm not angry at him, it's me. I've never ever acted that way, I mean I never asked a guy, so he should have said yes," I said, somewhat illogically. "Besides, now he thinks I'm always flinging myself at men in elevators when I'm drunk or high. I'm done with drugs, anyway."

"Drugs are a huge waste of money," Sue agreed. "But you'll run into him. Everyone meets everyone in New York—there aren't that many places to go, are there?"

She had a good point. Everyone I knew cycled through the same uptown museums, downtown bars, and art-house movie theaters. Meeting people was no big deal in Manhattan.

Soon enough, I spotted Jeremy standing in a movie line with a tall woman who wore a camel coat—they looked like two fashion models, ready for a shoot. I had imagined that Jeremy was trying to make up his mind about me, not dating gorgeous women in public places. But he had a right to date whomever, even if she was as pretty as a waitress.

Another girl might have fled, but I marched to the scene of the crime. "Jeremy, how have you been? You know, I've been kind of busy with the new job and everything, which is great because I needed a change of scenery." To his date, I said with a cheerful smile, "Jeremy and I used to work together sort of, only I wasn't very good at the work part of my job."

Jeremy looked shell-shocked. "You look thin, Bella," he said.

"It's the hot dog diet. It works, but only if you don't eat the buns, something to do with metabolism," I confided cozily to his companion, although she had no need for my friendly tip.

The camel coat-wearer was not sure if I was joking so, hedging her bets, she half-smiled. Jeremy looked at his loafers, avoiding me or trying to keep a straight face—I could not see which.

"Well, enjoy the film—*The Times* gave it a great review," I said and turned away before I turned beet-red and ruined my act. When I was safely across the street, I tried to check if they held hands, but by then, the line had moved.

Maybe it was then, maybe later that week, I made a decision. I did not mind Mr. Peterson: his stalwart attitude in the face of a dull career, his pleasantness, and his never-failing courtesy. To me, he was a role model in his own quiet way, as was Sue Olinsky in her efficient one. But his comment about graduate school had stuck with me. School was the obvious solution. In her future career, Sue would manage budgets, direct operations, or do other amazingly useful things, all of which seemed beyond my slender talents.

I made up my mind—I never listened to anyone and I was not about to start now. But there was one, and only one person, whom I needed to tell.

I called Jeremy first thing in the morning. When I suggested lunch, he said, "No, dinner, tonight. Let's go to Frere Jacques."

Of course, I accepted. And there we were.

A plump French waitress led us to a corner table, clucking with pleasure over Jeremy, as all women did. I noticed that all the French waitresses were matronly plump women—not skinny at all.

"I've been a dope, Bella," Jeremy said. He played with my fingers, bouncing them on the table.

"It's hard to time stuff," I said. "The girl at the movie—she was very pretty, and she had a nice camel coat. The two of you looked right together."

"I'll think I'll marry her because she has a nice camel coat. We can walk around together in matching camel coats. Maybe we'll buy matching hats, too."

"Anyway, I am an open-minded person," I said, affecting a breezy woman-of the-Riviera manner.

"Anyway, I am not," he said in a decidedly non-Riviera tone.

I remembered my loud comment about the stiletto-loving men. "You're not?" I asked.

He shook his head slowly, fixing his dark eyes on me to see how I took his news.

"So you're that kind of dope," I said, not unhappily.

He nodded "yes" emphatically.

"Oh," I said. "Well, I'm not really so open-minded. In fact, I'm kind of closed-minded, you know, actually extremely closed-minded—maybe even totally possessive. But how was I supposed to know that I was totally possessive when I've never been in love before, you see what I mean?"

"Yes," he said, still nodding.

"I'm thinking of going to grad school in maybe linguistics, maybe philosophy or something else, I'm not even sure what. I know, I have to take GREs and that takes time. It's just that I can't see myself doing this for years and years," I said. "It feels like the right decision, but…Jeremy, what are you doing?"

Jeremy's head was under the tablecloth. "I'm checking," he said. "And you are correct. The shoes are very sexy, very sexy." He stroked my leg until his hand hit the back of my knees.

I placed my hand on his before things got out of control. "I'm trying to be serious and practical and make plans—like I should learn to drive a car and I should know the cost of eggs. I should pay attention to things," I said.

He planted his head on the table and looked at me, wide-eyed and goofy. "Let's be serious. Let's be practical. What should we be practical about?"

"Do you think I'm doing the right thing? Leaving New York—quitting a job, going to grad school and well, not being here?" I did not add "with you," because I could not bear to say it aloud.

"I do," he said in his grown-up voice.

"Oh," I said, looking away in case I started crying and smearing my eyeliner.

"Bella, it's not that. I want you here but I think you could do anything you want to. You should be famous. And if you leave New York, I'll move or take a train or fly, because we'll figure it out and we have time and I love you." He kissed the inside of my wrist and then started kissing more. "Even your wrists are thin."

I whispered, "Not now, Jeremy, later."

"OK but eat some bread." He pushed the bread toward me, and I took one slice and then another. It was delicious, airy French bread.

"There is an actual bread diet," I told him. "Some French movie star lost tons of weight eating bread the way they do in Paris. She lived on bread for, I don't know, like years. Now it's a really famous diet. I guess it's kind of a prison diet now that I think about it."

"But it only works if you don't eat the hot dogs," said Jeremy.

# THREE

"There's a new theory that Jews and Irish are related—something to do with DNA," Sue Olinsky announced as we tirelessly removed every hyphen from the revised edition of *Principles of Refrigerating and Air Conditioning, Volume 21*.

It said much about my job that upon hearing the word Irish, my first thought was that potatoes must never, under any circumstances, be refrigerated. "Maybe so, but at least we don't inflict 'Danny Boy' on the general public," I said.

To my horror, the usually sane Sue began to croon that awful tune. It was, alas, a sure sign that her heart had been stolen by a man with smiling Irish eyes and nothing else. She removed her oversized eyeglasses and gazed at me, fluttering her eyelashes.

"Some guys say I look Irish," she declared.

As a luscious barmaid in Dublin, Sue might have found her groove. She might have worn low-cut dresses and gossiped with the lads, rather than squeezing her curves into a sexless pantsuit. Still, facts were facts, and seedy bars on Third Avenue were not, by any stretch of the imagination, colorful pubs in Dublin.

"Let me spare you years of psychotherapy," I said. "Jewish parents have Jewish children and not Irish ones. We don't get a parade down Fifth Avenue. Plus, no one, and I mean no one, ever talks about the luck of the Jews, and if they do, they are seriously misinformed."

"I can call myself OH-Linsky and who's the wiser," she pointed out as she killed another stubborn hyphen.

"A rose by any name is, uh, still a rose or whatever," I said.

Without missing a beat, Sue corrected me. "You mean, would smell as sweet." Sue would have done well on *Jeopardy!*

"Well, the guys you're meeting at the Pig in the Pen or O'Lunney's don't know Shakespeare and I doubt that they remember a girl's last name, much less her first."

She turned dreamy-eyed. "You're wrong. Tim was a real Irish musician and he said I was beautiful."

I returned to editing a dull article about the refrigeration of apples and pears, which, against all odds, went on for over fifty pages. But my mind failed to focus on the properties of autumnal fruits, and instead floated toward the word "beautiful" that had been bestowed on Sue Olinsky.

"Jeremy never says I'm beautiful," I said.

Sue tactfully lowered the bar. "Pretty?" she asked.

"No, either okay or fine," I admitted in a low voice. In my mind, "sexy" didn't count, at least not the way a word like "beautiful" did. Even "love" didn't fit the bill.

"Alcohol's what he needs," said Sue in problem-solving mode. She went on in a motherly fashion. "Bella, you can't expect a man who's stone-cold sober to start calling girls gorgeous, can you? A man needs a few drinks."

True, the chances of getting a fantastic compliment increased, and probably exponentially, with liquor. But I couldn't imagine Jeremy Levy, in his alligator polo shirts and Adidas, turning mellow or wobbly. "Jeremy doesn't drink. I need a different strategy," I said.

I met Jeremy later at an Upper West Side bar/restaurant, Aaron's Garden. The place was packed and noisy, no matter what the hour. It wasn't the most comfortable place, either. Tables were squeezed together, inches apart, and so in order to offer an illusion of spaciousness, all the walls were mirrored.

The mirrors did not lie. My hair flew in all directions, none of them good—and my dress, so deceptively slinky in a dressing room, was hideous in the extreme. A man would have to drink gallons, I thought sadly, and even then. Jeremy's hair, needless to say, was perfectly curled even after he'd come from tennis or basketball or another of his many sporting activities which I admired, albeit from afar. For my part, getting out of bed was exercise enough. On top of that, my heels were so high that I could barely walk, much less sprint.

"I hate my hair. I need to cut it!" I announced with sudden fierceness, as though I were about to go bald like the wild-eyed woman in *The Naked Kiss*. We had seen that film a few weeks earlier at a revival house.

He almost smiled and returned to reading the menu, although we always ordered the same hamburger or chicken salad.

A pert waitress with bangs took our order. With a flirty smile at Jeremy, she sashayed off to her next table, where six or seven bearded men were engaged in an angry debate about how to end world hunger. They calmed down, though, when presented with a large basket of fresh wholegrain breads.

I continued to stew about my unruly hair. When the waitress returned with root beer for Jeremy and wine for me, I said, "How do you get your bangs to hang so straight? My hair won't do that."

"Oh, my hair used to control me. It was a huge problem before auditions, but now, I am in complete control," she revealed. "I am the master of my hair." She exhaled, relieved to have conquered such a formidable enemy.

"You are," I marveled. Jeremy sipped his root beer through a straw, and his eyes became saucer-wide.

"I use Ben at Hair Aesthetics. Tell him Drew Hayworth sent you." She scribbled a phone number, with incredible rapidity, on my paper napkin. She knew it by heart.

"So I guess Ben's more than just your hairdresser?" I asked. It was reassuring that Drew Hayworth had no time for men like Jeremy, what with controlling her perfect hairdo and Ben, besides.

"It's complicated," the young Venus murmured and was off again.

"I wonder what exactly is complicated. Maybe it's a case of unrequited love or maybe they had a fight," I said to Jeremy.

"We may never know," he said with complete gravity. And then he kissed me in a decidedly non-joking way, which helped me forget about Drew's mysterious love life.

The next week, I persuaded Sue to accompany me to Hair Aesthetics. "I can't face the stress, especially when I'm taking the GREs soon. They'll have those tiny little squares or circles to fill out, and all those weird words like 'torpor,'" I said. "Plus, haircuts, you never know. They can go seriously wrong."

"It's too much stress," she agreed.

Hair Aesthetics was a third-floor walk-up on the Upper East Side way over toward York. On the stairwell, we bumped into a woman of unusual height whose thick locks fell asymmetrically over one eyebrow. With a heavy heart, I recognized her as one of *Vogue*'s giraffe-necked fashion models. "I probably can't afford this," I whispered to Sue. "I should have known that New York waitresses spend tons on their hair."

"This doesn't look like a legitimate salon," Sue opined loudly as we stumbled over stacks of hardcover books. "It needs a little sprucing up, in my opinion."

It was an odd-looking place, with antique chairs and ornate mirrors. But, with my newly acquired urban logic, I sensed that its shabby informality was intentional, and like torn jeans, distressed leather, and ripped T-shirts, a sign of ultimate cool.

Ben turned out to be a broad-shouldered six-footer with bright red hair and piercing blue eyes, looking more at home on the football field than in a chic hair salon. He took Sue's complaint in stride. "We didn't want a harsh corporate effect here. Haircuts can be traumatic," he said.

I wondered who the "we" was. The staff, so to speak, appeared to consist of Ben himself.

"We're not in the market for trauma," warned Sue.

Hearing Sue Olinsky's bossy tone, I expected Ben's dark or darker side to show. But he flashed what can only be described as a charming grin at her. "Benjamin Grace, at your service," he said, with a slight bow of his head.

Sue said, "Not mine, my friend's the one for the haircut. I use my mother's hairdresser in Brooklyn. I can't stop because it would hurt her feelings, even if she doesn't do the greatest job in the world, as you can see." She laughed one of her hearty ones and began exploring the books.

"Grace, that's an unusual name," I observed.

"Not in County Limerick," he said with the pleasure that his countrymen perennially exhibit toward their native land. "Let's move on to your hair. What do you want from it?"

I preferred to focus on other matters. "Haircutting isn't a very Irish sort of profession," I said.

"I'm half-Irish," he said by way of explanation. He lifted strands of my hair with a scrutiny that seemed vaguely clinical, and, adding to this medical aspect, covered me in a white gown. He continued his probe and asked, "Have you thought about what you want do with your hair?"

"Not really," I said. "But maybe it should lie flat and not fly around so much. Anyway, I met your, um, friend Drew at Aaron's Garden and I liked her hair."

Ben overlooked my Drew reference. "Maybe your hair is meant to fly around forever. We shouldn't fight that."

Sue emerged from her printed matter. "That's very poetic, Ben. Did you know there's a theory that the Jews and the Irish are related?"

"Absolutely," he said, and attacked my tresses with the confidence of a surgeon.

As hair fell to the floor, I distracted myself. "So, what's with Drew?"

Ben said, "She's a lovely girl, but she's an actress, and I don't see myself with an actress or a singer or a model. No, I can't see that." He applied some magical potion to my hair, which tamed it, at least for the moment.

After I paid, Ben handed longhaired Sue his card with a flourish. "For being such a good friend, a discount," he said. "That is, if your mother's hairdresser won't take offense."

"Thank you, Ben. I think I'll take you up on that," Sue replied in a sweetly demure voice, rather different from her usual. She carefully placed the card in her wallet.

"What's the other half, Ben?" I asked. "The half that's not Irish, I mean."

"Jewish, my mother's Jewish," said Ben Grace.

I looked pointedly at Sue. "We Jews say if your mother's Jewish, then you're really Jewish."

"I do know," said Ben. "I was raised Jewish. I'd say that my mother looked something like your friend Sue. In fact, I'd say that Sue's just the kind of girl my mother would like."

"Would she now?" said Sue with her best Irish lilt.

"She would," he said, and his eyes, if memory serves me well, were indeed smiling. I wisely decided to leave them to settle the point, preferably over candlelight and tinkling piano.

The walk downtown was hot and sticky. It had rained, and faint steam rose from the city sidewalks. In those days, the Upper East Side, near York that is, had elegant Hungarian and German cafés where tiny elderly people drank tiny cups of coffee with whipped cream and talked in their own language, worlds away from jeans and T-shirts.

Along the way, my interest in my hair, never profound, evaporated. It was only hair, and whether it stuck out or lay flat, what was the difference? I still had GREs to take and all that they implied. When I got home, I showered and undid all of Ben's artistry—and then I changed into shorts, T-shirt, and flip-flops. My hair was sopping wet when Jeremy rang the buzzer.

"Jeremy, I didn't expect you for hours," I said.

"I wanted to celebrate. I got a story published—it's a ghost story. I know, it's not the kind of thing you read," he said.

Men are deep. All this time, while I had imagined him playing basketball or reading Beckett, Jeremy had been writing about ghouls and monsters and ghosts. And he hadn't told me, or maybe I hadn't noticed.

"You're wrong, I love ghost stories," I said, draping my arms around him. "We should go out and have fun."

"I was thinking we'd have fun first and then go out." He kissed the nape of my now bare neck and then my ears. "Your hair's so short," he said.

"I got it cut. You're not going to believe it, but the hairdresser turned out to be Jewish but also Irish and straight. So he's perfect for Sue Olinsky, because she's kind of convinced that Irish and Jews are related. Plus, he likes Sue and not Drew because she's an actress and he doesn't want an actress or maybe his mother doesn't. I mean what are the chances?"

"Oh, one in ten," Jeremy said.

"So do you think I look okay? I went overboard, but I was in a bad mood and anyway, hair grows back."

It sounds silly, but I was almost on the verge of tears about nothing at all, absolutely nothing.

He played with my mouth, first making it frown, and then turning it into a version of a smile. "Don't worry so much about everything," he said.

I took a deep breath. "I'm trying, I really am trying."

He ran his hands all over me and kept on saying my name. And when there was no distance between us, he whispered lots of other things, stone-cold sober.

Afterward, I reached into my closet and found a flashlight, the sturdy kind you carry when the trail's dark and there are only the stars to guide you. I drew the shades to shut out the streetlights and spread a flowered sheet over us, even our faces—and I switched on the flashlight. All we could see was one another, lit up as if by a campfire.

"Now, tell me a story. But not the one you published—a new story that's just for me," I said.

He pressed me to him. "Oh, I have lots of those," he whispered.

"Just for me?"

He nodded as if we were playing Twenty Questions and he didn't want to give himself away too soon.

"And another thing," I told him. "I know those literary editors like the type of story where girls fling themselves out of windows and what have you, but I like a happy ending or one that makes you feel happy anyway."

His eyes were so grave and dark and he looked suddenly like a boy. "This girl flies to Mars," he said.

"That's a relief," I said. "I'm guessing she has superpowers and she meets a nice Martian boy and they zoom around the galaxy having fun and wearing cool spacesuits. But maybe I'm jumping ahead."

"Oh, you're a bonnie lass, you are," Jeremy said, and we started rolling around again, only this time with the flashlight on and my eyes open wide.

# FOUR

At my office farewell party, Sue announced that weddings bells were in the air for her and Ben Grace.

"Wow, that was a short courtship," I said.

"Ben thinks that men should get married when they're still madly in love and not after," explained Sue as she passed me a slice of frosted yellow cake. She gave me a pointed look, as though my days of sunshine and laughter were numbered.

Mr. Peterson, too, fixed his watery gaze on me. "I suppose that you'll be next, assuming the young man's inclined, and why shouldn't he be?"

He helped himself to a doubly thick slice since he, like most happy men, disdained dieting. Several of the married engineers on the floor, balancing paper plates and coffee cups, peered at me with excitement. I felt as if I were about to cheat a whole roomful of harmless men who wanted nothing more than a few weddings, or at least a few more wedding cakes. Office life was fairly dull without gossip and parties.

I replied, "It's not like we're not thinking about getting married. It's that we're thinking about other things. Like me leaving for Philadelphia and grad school and finding an apartment."

Sue's large hands flew upward, and I noticed that she wore a sparkling diamond engagement ring. "Jeremy could move with you. It would be cheaper. Philadelphia is hardly Antarctica."

"Please, if you're from Brooklyn, anything outside of New York is like Antarctica and anyway, where would he find another job in publishing?" I asked.

"The University Press, for one," Sue said, to my intense annoyance.

"Anyway, Jeremy doesn't want to get married, which is fine with me. Marriage isn't really on the radar now."

"He doesn't want to get married ever or he doesn't want to marry you?" she asked with Brooklynese bluntness. No one could ever accuse Sue Olinsky of diplomacy.

I cringed. It had taken over a year for Jeremy Levy to fall madly in love with me, not even counting the months that he didn't notice that I was on the same planet, or the ones when we'd stopped speaking to one another. And Ben Grace had fallen head over heels for sensible Sue in a day, love at first sight. When I looked at it that way, it was deflating, not that I longed for a man like Ben, or even a wedding.

"If Jeremy wants to avoid marriage, the 'me' element is superfluous and maybe even illogical," I said, as though I were cutting through the thorny intellectual brambles.

"Not at all," argued razor-sharp Sue Olinsky, ever ready for a battle of brainpower. "A man could want to get married, but maybe he hasn't found the right wife. Maybe he wants a wife who's super-neat and his girlfriend's messy. That's a problem, especially when they say that most couples argue about housework. That's the number one argument."

Everyone looked toward my desk, a virtual disaster of paper and fashion magazines and file folders. Several engineers recoiled in horror.

"I am very messy," I confessed.

"I only used messy as an example. Some men might want a thrifty wife, since money ranks number two," Sue said in a consoling tone.

Sue's prowess in the money-saving department was the stuff of office legend. She cagily clipped coupons for laundry detergent and shampoo from the Sunday paper. Meanwhile, I was off buying the organic, overpriced versions at some out-of-the-way health food store on 13th Street, and if there was ever a sale, I was sure to miss it.

"My Ellen's great with budgets," said one of the young, plump engineers. He licked the white icing and smiled at me as if to lift my personal thriftiness to his wife's level.

"Hmm, if I had lots of money—which is kind of unlikely since I'm always broke—I'd spend it," I told him. "Actually, I'd spend it even if I only had a little money, and probably faster, since if you have only a little it goes quickly. Plus, in grad school, I won't have any money, so I won't have much to budget."

I laughed to show how little it all meant in the Grand Scheme of Life.

"Bella's on her way to graduate school," said Mr. Peterson as if to explain my housekeeping deficiencies. He looked as indulgent as any parent might, and I was grateful once again for his chivalry. Mr. Peterson was one in a million.

"Better marry a rich man," this plump bookkeeper of a man warned as he downgraded my matrimonial prospects from slender to bleak. He shuffled away, perhaps to find more free food. With the ever-thrifty Ellen as his spouse, he might be forced to haul foodstuffs of all kinds back home. Poor guy probably carried little paper bags filled with sticky leftover donuts or half of a ham sandwich on the subway to Queens.

"Jeremy's not rich and his place is much messier than mine. Chances are that no sensible woman wants to marry him," I confided.

"*Men* aren't supposed to be neat or thrifty," Sue said.

Mr. Peterson, no doubt both neat and thrifty, coughed quietly to make himself known. "Not all men, certainly," he commented with a timid smile.

"Your wife's a lucky woman," I assured him. To me, he was a hero of sorts, even if unfailing pleasantness earned him no medals.

"I don't think my parents thought about housekeeping or money when they got married. They were kind of in a hurry."

"That was the war," said Mr. Peterson rather gravely, as if the tragedy of Pearl Harbor was to force messy wives upon unsuspecting soldiers.

With the mention of military action, the party ground to a halt. The manly workers drifted off with their plates of cake and best wishes to Sue and dire thoughts about my unmarried and impoverished future.

When the coast was clear, I asked Sue, "Why the secret about you and Ben?"

"I've been wearing my ring for weeks, but you never asked. I thought you were jealous or something."

I wanted to make a joke, but it stuck in my throat. It was the first time I saw myself from the outside, as I appeared to women like Sue. To her, I was waiting for a diamond ring. I was waiting for something, but it wasn't for anything I could put my finger on.

# FIVE

"Why?" was Jeremy's confused response to hearing about Sue and Ben. I wasn't sure if he felt it odd that these two specific persons should wed, or whether he felt that marriage itself was a tribal ritual, practiced only by unthinking primitives like Ben and Sue.

"Ben says it's better now than later, and also, Sue's thrifty and neat, and Ben isn't," I explained. Judging from Jeremy's blank expression, my logic escaped him.

I held up one of my cherished favorites, a 1940s vintage dress with bright red cherries and a sequined belt. The wedding was in the remote future, but never too soon to think about what to wear. I asked, "Do you like this one?"

"No," he said, briefly raising his head from the small pillow. There was no place to sit and read, so we read in bed.

I held up another, a charmer with tiny rhinestones around its Peter Pan collar. He nodded, no, this time rather decisively.

"Don't you like anything?" I asked. I felt like one of those women in *Cosmopolitan*, in search of men's unpredictable whims: their fabled love of black fishnet stockings, violently purple nails, and so on.

"I like what you're wearing," he smiled and pulled me to him. Since I was wearing an antique slip and nothing else, that ended that, at least for a few happy hours.

Next morning, we were off to my parents" house in South Jersey. Packing was a trying business, since Jeremy's place was a peculiar mix of bareness and clutter. Not much furniture to speak of, but every surface occupied: tables covered with newspapers, dirty plates and ancient cartons of milk; bare floors served as the resting place for socks, pants, towels, and piles of poetry books, not to mention balls of dust. Both of his chairs—there were only two—were taken by a tennis racket and a basketball, respectively.

"You need chairs," I observed.

Jeremy's hand dropped to retrieve stray reading matter on the floor where, in his mind, books and newspapers belonged. He tilted his head toward the two pathetic specimens.

"I meant real chairs. You know, leather armchairs or something with wood or upholstery. These are what people have before they get real chairs." I almost added: These are what single guys have before they have a girlfriend, but that bordered on verbal conflict.

"I'm in the pre-chair phase," he replied.

This meeting would be Jeremy's introduction to my parents, or vice versa. I'd delayed it as long as I could, and managed to avoid Thanksgiving, Christmas, Labor Day, birthdays, you name it. Finally, I'd chosen an average summer weekend, the most average that I could find—lifting all pressures to decorate the house, roast a turkey, or buy gifts. It didn't take much to send my parents into a panicked, frenzied state, screaming.

"All you need to do is pick us up at the bus station. Nothing else, promise not to do anything," I told them over the phone.

"Don't get so nervous, honey," my father said. "Everything will be fine."

"Or it won't," said my mother, mournfully.

Jeremy clasped my hand tightly the entire bus ride. He knew that I dreaded the meeting, and, besides, the Greyhound bus was a true freezer. On the other end, I spotted Dad in one of his Hawaiian shirts, blue and pink, flowers and sailboats, and my mother in one of her denim shirtwaists, the kind that are perennially out of fashion.

Alongside them stood a small red-haired boy, with huge glasses and pale freckles. I gave him a big hug, which he pretended not to like.

My mother announced: "We're taking care of Mo today. His mother has studying to do."

My father laughed loudly, as he did when nothing was funny, and led us to the Chevy. He took in Jeremy's polo shirt and loafers and shook his hand heartily. My mother murmured, "So you are Jeremy." She sounded as if she had expected someone older or taller.

Pint-sized Mo turned to Jeremy with a baleful stare. "Who are you?" he demanded.

Jeremy stood with his arm around me. "Jeremy," he said, with a sober nod.

"Jeremy is Bella's new friend," my mother said. "He is her friend." The way she said "friend," it sounded like she was translating from the Swahili.

Mo's interrogation went on. "Are you married?" he asked with a Puritanical expression. He had become prim for one so young.

"Is someone getting married?" asked my father, waking up. "Who, may I ask?"

I kneeled down to Mo's level. "I'm waiting for Mo. I can't marry anyone else." We giggled together, and I brushed his soft pink cheek. "Oh, you are dashing, you are."

"No one's getting married," my mother said, lips pursed.

I tried to introduce a cheery note into the discussion. "My friend Sue Olinsky's getting married," I said. "The guy is someone she met through me. I'm sort of the Cupid in that romance and maybe I'll be the maid of honor."

I added that last bit to spice things up, since it was not, strictly speaking, true. But in the present circumstances, I felt that diversionary tactics were in order.

"Good. Someone's getting married," she replied. Conversation ceased, but the drive from the station was, thankfully, brief.

My parents had painted their house in a shade of green that they insisted was authentic Williamsburg, or some colony. The lawn (so-called) consisted of brownish weeds tall enough to approximate a cornfield, and a few tall oaks whose branches had fallen everywhere. On either side, their neighbors' front yards were neatly edged with trim circular hedges and colorful flowerbeds, their lawns a shimmering emerald green. In fact, all along the street, every lawn was manicured and framed by a freshly painted white fence—a picture postcard, except for my parents' house.

"Maybe you should hire some kids to do the lawn," I suggested fancifully.

"That is an insane suggestion," said my mother. "That is completely insane." She stooped to pluck a weed or two as if putting the finishing touches on an otherwise perfect canvas. "I hate a formal look," she added proudly.

"It looks fine, Mom, really it does," I said. "I'm glad we're here, and I'm glad to see Mo, too."

Mo said to me, eyes shining, "I have an earthworm collection. They are really creepy and slimy! I keep them here because my mom won't let me keep them because they are disgusting." He rushed to retrieve his treasure and returned with a large worm-filled glass jar—clearly, master of the house. "Here, look!" he said, thrilled.

One glance at the two adjacent houses told me that their owners wouldn't put up with a boy like Mo. Rational women like Mo's mom disliked bugs and dirt and worms, and punished kids who brought them inside.

I said, "Oh, they're very special. They are important to the wetlands, right?"

He shook his small head in eager agreement. Then he approached Jeremy with his jar and looked up at him with a boy's reverence. "Do you want to see my worms?" he asked as if offering a rare treat.

Jeremy barely registered Mo. "Later," he said.

My mother took Mo by his small shoulders and steered him inside. I could hear her whispering, "No talking about worms before lunch. Poor Jeremy, you're spoiling his appetite. He is from Brooklyn, where they don't have any worms, and people are very scared of them."

I waited for Jeremy to contradict her. Instead, he took my arm and headed inside, oblivious to everything but me, and I felt hot and cold at once. I wanted everyone to see Jeremy as I did, when we were alone, and I was at the center of everything. But the truth was, it wasn't just marriage that was off Jeremy's radar, it was people.

I'd had a start of a headache on the bus, and now the light hurt, the way it does before a migraine, and I felt even less steady. I left Mo and Jeremy with my father, and wandered into the kitchen to make coffee, as if everything were fine. My mother hovered as I prepared coffee, always on guard for my migraines.

"You should take a nap," she said—sleep being her all-in-one solution for all of life's troubles. "You look very tired."

"I can't sleep now," I snapped. "Anyway, coffee will help. It's stress. Once I find an apartment in Philly and get settled in grad school, I won't be so up in the air and in-between everything, I'll feel relaxed. I'll be settled."

She shook her head slowly. "So Jeremy will be in New York, and you'll be in Philadelphia for four years—and what is getting settled? I don't understand."

"No one's asking you to understand," I said, and then wished I hadn't.

"I wasn't trying to argue," she answered in her martyred voice. "But four years is a long time for any couple, a very long time."

I waited for the coffee. I thought: No one ever tries to argue, they just do. No one walks into a room, unless they're lawyers, and wonders how to start a fight. But people end up fighting just the same as if they'd been planning it for their entire lives. People could get advanced degrees in finding fault with others.

"Five years is more like it," I said.

"He's a handsome boy, Jeremy," she said, as though she were following a thread. "And I see he's a little shy, which isn't such a terrible thing in my mind. Does he want coffee, too?"

"No, he doesn't drink coffee or tea," I said. "Plus, he doesn't have any chairs, except yellow folding chairs which are impossible to sit on. It's ridiculous."

My mother eyed me cautiously, and I felt that I'd said something out of line. Then she said, "Bella, if a man doesn't have chairs, he needs a woman to help him buy some. He doesn't need her to live in another apartment in another city with her own chairs. Besides, I have lots of extra chairs that you could take if you were so bothered by something like a chair, which is not something normal people get bothered about."

"I didn't say I was bothered. I was making a simple statement of fact, an observation if you will," I said.

I met her eyes to make it clear that I wasn't about to go shopping for Jeremy's chairs or anyone else's. Love hadn't made me neat or thrifty. It hadn't made me anything except happy, but it was a stripped-down, no-frills version of happy—just the basics, no chairs.

"Nothing's simple with you. Have you met Jeremy's parents?" asked my mother as she aimlessly wiped the counter, without any apparent results.

"Here, let me," I said, grabbing the pink sponge from her and scrubbing the Formica counter with more vigor. "Not yet. Jeremy's parents live pretty far away in Brooklyn. It's a long train ride back to the Upper West Side." I tried my best to sound convincing, since she knew as well as I did that Brooklyn is right next to Manhattan—plus, how difficult is it to take a train?

"I didn't know Jews of my generation still lived in Brooklyn. Everyone we knew moved out to Jersey or the Island or Westchester, after the war. I guess a few Jews stayed behind," she said, which, translated, meant that the Jews with ambition or money moved out, so that left the "other kind" stranded in Brooklyn.

"Yes, amazing as it seems, there are Jews in Brooklyn," I said. "It's extraordinary, but they are there, not even counting the Lubavitchers. There are dentists and doctors and accountants and teachers. There is a whole borough."

"True, a tree still grows in Brooklyn," she sighed, and I laughed. "I'll give you chairs for your new apartment. You could take the Thonets or the wicker, and there's that beautiful American Gothic chair, and a Victorian loveseat too. It will be so beautiful."

I gave her the kiss that I should have offered her at the bus station. "Don't worry, Mom, I'll figure it out," I told her.

"Or you won't," she said.

# SIX

Center City Philadelphia looked as transient as a Greyhound bus station: empty sidewalks, a block-sized Salvation Army store, porn shops, and bars for real drunks, not wild, fun-loving college kids. Still, it had a faded thrift store grandeur. Once-beautiful Victorians that were cut up into cramped apartments for students who, as soon as they graduated, fled for L.A. or Manhattan, and left stuff on the curb: torn sofas, soiled mattresses, broken toasters, aged file cabinets. It wasn't rich people's junk, the way it was on the Upper East Side, just garbage. But, compared to New York, Philly was dirt-cheap, plus I had a full stipend. I felt richer in grad school than I had working in publishing.

Fall semester started with an invitation to an "Opening Reception," which sounded grand to me, or grand enough to don one of my vintage dresses (one that Jeremy, perhaps prophetically, had rejected) and while I was at it, red lipstick and high heels.

Thus attired, I entered a roomful of fresh-faced flannel-clad women, who might have flown in from the pages of *L.L. Bean* or maybe an Amish farm. Where, I wondered, were all the sexy intellectuals? Maybe they lingered in a nearby bistro discussing Descartes over a bottle of wine, or perhaps they'd arrive fashionably late, having first stopped at the campus bookstore to browse through the latest copy of *Le Monde* or *Der Spiegel*.

"For the record, low heels are OK, but lipstick, not so much," said a fellow student whose nametag read "Jessica Tang."

More problematic, all the women I saw were named Kirsten, Kristen, Kristy and Katrin, which defied the odds. I whispered, "What is this, one of those weird social psychology experiments where we'll get tested about whose names we recall?"

"Plus all these new women are super-thin, and I am feeling huge," moaned Jessica. "These jeans make me feel fat, but you don't have to worry about that."

"I used to feel fat too before I went on the Eating Less Diet. You only eat half of what's on your plate, and then you're not as fat," I explained.

"Hmm, forget that. Between psych, linguistics, sociology, poli sci and communications, there's free food pretty much every day, and who has the money to buy food?" she replied. "Speaking of which, there's a talk on Whorf versus Chomsky this week. That department has a great wine and cheese reception."

"Didn't Chomsky win that debate decades ago?" I asked.

Jessica shook her head to disabuse me of such youthful hopes. "Number One Rule in academia: No debate is ever done. You name it, it's going strong—nature-nurture, mind versus matter, whatever. They go on and on and just get nastier and nastier." She waved toward a few mild-mannered and harmless-looking men and women. "These guys detest one another. It's a low-level war zone."

"I think most people hate each other, so it's OK," I said. "What's Rule Number Two?"

At which point, a tall woman sidled over to us. She was wearing a distressed black leather jacket and knee-high black boots and fell definitely into the brainy-sexy column. Upon close inspection, I recognized her from the school bulletin as Professor Natasha Lowenstein, whose latest book was *Reading as Politics,* or was it *Politics as Reading?* When I got nervous, my brain turned into a virtual spaghetti strainer.

I said, "I saw your book the other day in a bookstore and I almost bought it."

"It's not a page-turner," she murmured as she grabbed more than a few shrimps. She seemed oddly indifferent to my reading preferences, but it seemed rude to agree with her.

"I'm sure it's worth reading," I replied with as much conviction as I could muster. Surely an author took pride in her own life's work?

Natasha's sly grin suggested otherwise. "I doubt it. Jessica can give you the CliffsNotes version. But you come and talk to me very soon, Bella."

She was off to dazzle other students. Jessica blinked. "I took her courses when I was an undergraduate and she is so brilliant. Isn't she amazing? I mean, isn't she so incredibly, well, incredible?" She sighed theatrically as if to suggest how hopeless it was.

"Ahem, aren't you a student?" I asked, although I might have asked, isn't she a professor? Either way, Jessica's prospects looked slim to none. She was likely to have competition in the Dr. Natasha Lowenstein department from men, women, transgender, you name it. Natasha had what you call "charisma."

"That's Rule Number Two, or least that's what she says, but it's just an excuse," said Jessica, despairing. "I've heard a rumor that she's secretly married to Sky Lowe, the film director, you know, the guy who did *Kill More or Die!*"

"I loved *Kill More or Die!*" I squealed and looked around guiltily. I wasn't sure whether my love of gory action films was permitted in the hallowed halls of academe. "I mean, it was fun, wasn't it?"

"Definitely, so how am I supposed to compete with that?" complained Jessica.

In a few minutes, I learned the saga of Jessica Tang. As an undergrad, Jessica had run around with guys who were aging artists, campus drug dealers, and other undesirables. "It was one late-night tear-fest after another: how could he, why did he, and any longer, I'd have joined a cult or ended up sobbing my heart out on an afternoon talk show. Anyway, my parents were relieved when it turned out that I liked women. Plus, Natasha Lowenstein is smart, which my mother likes, even though she may be married."

"My boyfriend, Jeremy, is smart and my parents aren't jumping for joy. I would call them joyless, where he's concerned," I confessed.

Jessica snatched a few devilled eggs from a passing tray, and passed another to me, which I delicately refused. "But he is single," said Jessica, munching on an egg.

"Exactly. My parents think he shouldn't be," I said.

"What kind of sick parents do you have?" asked Jessica, aghast. She availed herself of some more shrimp to calm her spirits, and then added more eggs.

"Please, keep it clean! My parents think Jeremy should marry me," I said.

"That kind of married," she said, exhaling. "But you just started the program. Getting married now doesn't make sense."

"If you think mothers make sense, you haven't met mine," I said. "Anyway, it's not as if I'm dying to get married. But I'd like him to say things, like when we buy a house, or when we have a car. I'd like him to imply marriage like it's a given, even if it isn't."

"Of course!" said Jessica with much feeling.

"And he doesn't ever say anything, ever. Although to be fair, he doesn't talk at all."

"He's a mute?"

"No, he's a writer," I said.

"Oh, he's a writer! No wonder you want to get married. Picture, please, now."

I wearily pulled out a photo of me and Jeremy entwined, me in an ugly kaftan, and Jeremy in jeans and a white T-shirt, looking *GQ*-perfect as usual. I was used to the public response to any picture of the two of us.

"My hair usually doesn't look that frizzy," I noted somewhat inaccurately. "Sometimes I blow it dry and it looks a little better."

"Forget your hair, his looks fine," said Jessica in awestruck tones. "Why have you left this Adonis in New York?"

"Believe it or not, Jeremy never notices other women," I said. And seeing Jessica's raised eyebrows, I added, "And I don't notice other men."

"If you say so," said Jessica.

# SEVEN

Maybe you can't go home again, but you can always go back to school. I loved the familiar feel of musty-smelling libraries, lined paper notebooks, hours of homework, even bad food. All the grad students ate at a nearby deli. Its décor—steel tables, linoleum floor, greying walls—was drab, its coffee weak, but it was cheap. I limited myself to a single scoop of cottage cheese, with dry whole-wheat toast, and Lipton's tea.

"School is like summer camp compared to editing articles about the storage of Russet potatoes," I said over what I called lunch. "Turns out that if all you do is study, you know way more than other people. It's not linear, though. Like if you study ten times as much, you know maybe, say, twice as much."

"Well, that's why Natasha likes you," said Jessica, returning to her large meatball sub. "I'm just a gay Asian-American female to her. That is all I am, all I will ever be."

"You are a gay Asian-American female," I was forced to point out. Actually, most of the graduate program was gay. I was an outlier, a token straight woman.

She glowered at me. "I meant, just another gay Asian-American female."

Almost any day of the week offered a lecture with, as Jessica had promised, tasty wine and cheese receptions, limited to persons of stunning seriousness, often of the black turtleneck species. In those days, the rage was talks that deconstructed another, more famous, theory. I guess that professors had run out of their own theories, and were resigned to deconstructing others, because after all, there's only so much to say.

That afternoon, the featured speaker was a British woman who had published dozens of books on language theory, and who, after a quarter century at Berkeley, still spoke in a plummy British accent no longer found on the streets of London. With her cropped hair and sensible shoes, she was an academic Mary Poppins.

"To quote Whorf," she began.

Everyone offered a friendly nod, as if the very mention of Whorf soothed an old grievance. Freud, Darwin, Marx, Chomsky, the more names, the more nods—some names elicited melancholy sighs or sharp guffaws. Everyone took reams of notes, although the speaker's thoughts were sadly limited to two. These two ideas were recycled over the course of an hour, in the manner of an annoying relative who has exhausted all topics and must run on about her health. But I enjoyed listening to her accent, which made her sound so clever.

As the Q&A arrived, I was lost in contemplation of how I, too, might acquire a tony accent or just a trace of one to up my profundity quotient. I pictured myself, index finger on chin, wearing thick-rimmed black eyeglasses and a dove-grey pleated skirt. No, perhaps a black leather jacket, somewhat weather-beaten, with a slender black pencil skirt. That would suit me better.

My pleasant fashion reverie was abruptly interrupted by Natasha. She prodded me and said, "Bella, you might ask a question now. This is a good time."

Her definition of a good time seemed questionable. The speaker's two thoughts had failed to strike a chord with the audience. By now, more than a few eyelids were drooping. I couldn't very well solicit fashion advice. In truth, my mind was empty. An hour's worth of "therefore" and "let us consider" had placed me into a trance-like state, bordering on slumber.

But I'd absorbed a few of Natasha's rhetorical techniques, which boiled down to repeating whatever the speaker's topic was in question form. Thus armed, I asked as if struggling to express a buried thought. "I am confused…do you agree with Chomsky?" I saw many bobs of the head in the audience. Natasha looked as if a pet rabbit had performed a trick.

The speaker's eyes lit up. "You *have* been paying attention," she said.

Without missing a beat, she launched into a rather obscure set of examples, involving John Donne, Ferraris, and the Theory of Relativity, which managed to circumvent the question entirely. From that point on, the room became animated, almost ferocious, as one theory of language battled another. Jessica was correct: Any idea, no matter how moldy, was granted eternal life in academia. There must have been an Angel of Discarded Theories at every conference and colloquium, beaming kindly upon the never-ending debates.

I made a mental note to tell Jeremy. Only he would get the joke, I thought, and I suppressed a giggle. And then, I saw an older man, but not too old, smile at me—it seemed that he got the joke, too. He was tall, very thin, with a full mouth, and he wore an oversized dark sweater of the type worn by men in French New Wave cinema.

At the inevitable wine and cheese reception, Natasha introduced the tall man as Francois Morel, from Cognitive Psychology. Francois and I were in parallel fields and, in Natasha's words, "were bound to meet."

"And you, do you agree with Chomsky?" asked Francois in a sweet way, as if he wanted to know my answer. It was rare to hear a pure question and not a challenge.

"Of course, the structure of language has to be related to how we think. But that's the boring part—it's universal, so it's by definition not exciting. Vocabulary, irony, wit, dialect, jokes, those are learned, that's what I'm interested in," I said. "I grew up hearing Yiddish, which isn't German, but it's an overlay on it. It's got these amazing words."

"But learning vocabulary, that's related to how the mind works," said Francois. "A dolphin can't learn different words for the same thing, but humans can learn ivory and white and alabaster. Milky white and snowy white."

"If you're going to go that route, then everything's a function of general intelligence, so why bother studying anything except the brain?" Natasha asked, dismissively.

"That's one way to look at it," he replied with a good-natured smile.

"Obviously, Francois and I don't agree on much, but you should take his course. It's useful," said Natasha to me. "We need to understand our intellectual enemies—no offense Francois."

"None taken," he said, staring at me. I noticed that he wore a wedding ring, which should not have mattered as much as it seemed to. He said, "I hope you will take my seminar next semester."

"It depends on my schedule. You see, I avoid classes on Fridays because my boyfriend's in New York, so I leave early for the weekend." I spoke as though I had to defend my dating rights from invading foreign professors.

"Ah, New York," said Francois, glossing over the boyfriend part in favor of the glories of the Chrysler Building and Central Park. "We go to the Met to hear opera, do you?" he asked as if opera were as everyday as bagels.

"I wish, but that's way too expensive," I said.

Well, that was half true. The other half was that Jeremy liked the Yankees and horror movies, and probably never had listened to a single opera in his life and never wanted to.

Francois put down his wine glass. "My wife and I have a subscription to the Met, and we can't always use our tickets. There's a concert coming up that we have to miss, a performance of *Figaro*. You and your boyfriend, you can go. Don't say you can't accept. I insist. Write down your name, and I'll leave it at your department mailbox."

Natasha interjected, "My brother and I caught Levine's *Cosi* last season." She mentioned a strange name who had sung the "tenor" role and a few others. I made a note: Learn names of all famous tenors, sopranos and conductors, probably widely available in *The New York Times* music reviews.

"I can't thank you enough," I said. I printed my name in large bold letters, all capitals, with the words, "OPERA TICKETS" as if he would forget why he wanted my name.

Francois took the piece of paper from me and seemed vaguely amused. "Bella is a lovely name. Well, Bella, you will have to give me a long and highly entertaining review afterwards. Natasha can tell you where my office is—I'm usually there."

Natasha laughed, "That's putting it mildly. I'm surprised you're here now."

"Professional courtesy," explained Francois. "I must go home now. My wife's having a small dinner party…do you like to cook?" His comment was directed at me—and unless you counted tuna melts, cooking was not my specialty.

"Not exactly, maybe scrambling eggs," I said. I figured it was wise to omit the tuna-cheddar melts on English muffin, delicious though they were. I imagined that Madame Morel whipped up delicate trout dishes with those creamy dill sauces, which never made French women gain weight. Happily, *The New York Times* had many recipes along with the opera reviews, so I could clip them at the same time.

"Scrambled eggs, that's a nice light dinner, maybe a salad and red wine." He spoke with such enthusiasm that I figured he must be starved. It was getting late.

"That sounds nice, except for the red wine, which gives me a migraine," I said. "Most wine gives me a headache, so maybe just the eggs and the salad."

"You are not drinking the right wines, I think," said Francois.

Natasha, too, nodded gravely, and muttered what sounded like the names of choice wines for my benefit—although her expertise was lost on me, my knowledge of wine being limited to red and white, unless you counted Passover wine as a vintage.

I sighed, "You're probably correct."

Apart from gourmet cooking and knowledge of tenors, I'd also have to learn about fine wine—what next? I wondered. Academia was getting a little perplexing.

"You will learn," he told me as he put on his coat—cashmere, from the looks of it. He gave me a smile that I can only describe as enigmatic and was off.

The very next day, Francois Morel left me two tickets to *The Marriage of Figaro*, along with a handwritten note on ivory paper: Dear Bella, I await your review, F. Morel.

# EIGHT

Well, it was, as the poet says, a tangled web. Only one day after he had left me the opera tickets, Francois Morel sent a recording of *The Marriage of Figaro*. It arrived without his name. But it had its intended effect. I listened to Mozart and thought of how music and love are, often as not, intertwined; and like it or not, I had my first secret from Jeremy.

It might be hidden from Jeremy, but not, alas, from anyone else. In fact, I couldn't stop going on about Francois Morel. By now, my tolerant friends knew the entire intrigue (slender as it was) backward and forward. Naturally, Sue Olinsky had not escaped.

"It almost seems like cheating," I whispered to Sue as we shopped for her wedding gown.

We found ourselves in a dimly lit bridal shop in Brooklyn, called Elaine's Bridal, where Sue's aunt had worked. It couldn't have been a lark since the owner, Elaine, was an unsmiling woman of about sixty who seemed fed up with the whole wedding business. She seemed to have pegged me as an adulteress even before my Big Day.

"You need help?" she asked as though I were about to steal a groom or perhaps a gown. I obviously had not made a good impression.

"I'm not the one getting married. My friend is." I smiled at her in a vain attempt to repair my brand.

"None of my business who's getting married and who isn't," said Elaine. "It's a free country is what I say, and people can do as they please." She seemed to tolerate rather than encourage our presence in her empty store, for she was deeply engrossed by an article in *People*.

Sue explained whose niece she was and added, "I waited too long to shop for a dress, and now I have to find one. I hate shopping."

Elaine lifted her head reluctantly, as if receiving one more piece of bad news. She pointed to a few racks of satin dresses, some with faded brown spots from bridal seasons past, others puffy-sleeved and awful. I noticed more than a few dry-cleaning tags: did brides return their gowns afterwards?

"I got plenty of gowns, every style, for every type of figure," she said. She pulled out a garment of ungainly proportions. We almost fled at the sight of the big shiny dress.

"My friend needs something that pleases the groom. He is not fond of the shepherdess look. You see, he is foreign," I explained.

Elaine nodded with cynical understanding. "Oh, if he's foreign, you can never tell."

"Exactly, he wants less frills, less puffiness, less beads…well, less, less of everything," I said.

"A bride should have a little glitz. It's her big day, after all," Elaine complained. She held the dress higher as if to display its unseen virtues, but it looked worse when shown to full advantage. I pitied the poor bride stuck in all those layers, like a walking wedding cake.

"No glitz," I said. "My friend needs to see the simplest dress that you have, and she doesn't want to pay a lot. Less is more, if you get my drift."

"Like I say, the customer's always right," sighed Elaine, bitterly. She produced a blameless item that was not puffy, beaded, or anything remotely theatrical. "This is so plain that a nun could wear it, if a nun had a wedding. It's so plain it's hardly a wedding dress. You could even use it for your second wedding, it's so plain."

"One wedding is enough for me," said Sue as she grabbed the nun-like dress.

Elaine shrugged, "I wanted one wedding too, but go figure, I had three. Three weddings, three receptions. It's time-consuming, not to mention the expense."

We nodded in astonishment that three different men had voluntarily marched down the aisle with this harpy. "That is a lot of weddings," I said.

"You're telling me," said the three-timer.

I produced a fake-cheery chuckle. "I hope three's the lucky number!"

"Not really," answered Elaine as she returned to her *People*.

After a few minutes, Sue emerged from her dressing room a new woman. Even she had to pause and admire her sleek reflection. She double-checked the price.

"I'll take it," she told Elaine. And to me, she said, "Now, you have to promise to come to my wedding, and don't even think about bringing some French guy." She slapped my back and gave one of her big belly laughs, which startled even the unflappable Elaine.

"His name is Francois Morel," I said, when I had recovered from the blow.

"Another foreigner," said Elaine with a resigned expression.

I was about to explain but decided that, once again, less was more. If Elaine thought me a sinner or a temptress, so be it. I patiently waited for the two of them to conclude their elaborate, and it seemed endless, plans for the gown.

Sue and I hopped on a subway back to the Upper West Side— where we got on, the train was empty. I naturally returned to the drama of the opera tickets. "It's tricky. Jeremy's not much of an opera guy, but if I don't tell him, he might buy tickets to a game. But if I do tell, and say the word 'Francois'…who knows?" I lamented as we settled into the hum of the subway.

"You have to tell him," said Sue. "Opera can't compete with sports, no way."

"Problem is, Jeremy is kind of a mind reader. Not that I have anything to hide, but…" My thoughts wandered because the subway car was plastered, from one end to the other, with advertisements for Cheap Divorce Lawyers in Spanish, Korean, Mandarin, Tagalog, and, astonishingly, even in English.

"It's simple. You stress the 'free' part and you downplay the 'opera' part. Everyone loves getting free stuff," Sue said. "Say you won the tickets in a raffle, like in a school contest. Everyone likes winning contests, almost as much as they like 'free.'"

"But I didn't win anything. They were a gift."

Sue looked at me as she often did, as though I were an inpatient at Bellevue. "This is better than true. It's an improved version of true. You got the tickets for free, right? And it was pure luck, wasn't it? You didn't beg this French guy for tickets, he offered them. It was chance that you met, so there's no need to mention him at all."

"And I haven't spoken to him since," I said, trying to avoid the leering eyes of the Cheap Divorce Lawyers.

"Maybe, but boyfriends don't want to hear that sexy French guys are hanging around school, flirting, and handing out opera tickets. You need a neutral way to broach the subject, like, 'Wow, aren't we lucky? I won these opera tickets, and they usually cost hundreds of dollars, but they're free!' It's easy," said Sue, who did make it sound easy, which it probably was if you were Sue Olinsky.

On the walk back from the subway, I stopped to pick up Jeremy's favorite black-and-white cookies. The bakery on 86th had its usual line out the door—rain or shine, New Yorkers craved sweets. Inside, I saw a familiar-looking couple—I couldn't place them, though—staring ahead in angry silence.

"One black-and-white," murmured the male as the female fixed her stony glance downward. I gave the beleaguered guy a shrug of sympathy, like a fellow soldier in arms. And as I did, I recognized him: Sky Lowe, the movie director of *Kill More or Die!*

not to mention his reputation as lover or perhaps spouse of Professor Natasha Lowenstein.

So my tangled web, so to speak, was mingled with the thrill of an unexpected celebrity sighting. "You can't believe who I just saw buying black-and-white cookies!" I squealed to Jeremy, who was immersed in a basketball game.

"No, I can't," he said.

"Sky Lowe, the *Kill More or Die!* director, and he was with a woman, which means he's probably not Natasha's secret husband, which means Jessica has a chance, and by the way, I won two free opera tickets in some sort of raffle, so we can go to the Met for free," I said.

"You never mentioned liking opera," he said. He gave me a faintly sinister glance.

Now, Jeremy and I weren't one of those sophisticated New York couples who chat about the Death of the Novel or what's new in Mideast politics. We had what might be called the minimalist approach to sharing: I knew nothing of basketball, and he nothing of social science. Yet here he was, speculating about my preferences in vocal music.

I said loftily, "It's a new interest of mine. So this will be something different."

Jeremy said, "Oh, it will be." He grabbed the black-and-white cookie to go with his milk.


Back at school, Jessica Tang took a dim view of my duplicity. "You will live to regret this," she warned. "Lying's never good."

"I regret it already, but what do I say? Hey, there wasn't a contest? That would sound seriously stupid. It would seem like I'm hiding something, which I am, but I'm not, since there's nothing to hide."

"I'd never lie to Natasha. Not that she'd care, since she doesn't know I exist," said Jessica.

"Jessica, how could Natasha not know, when you're always following her around looking lovesick or just plain sick? And I forgot to tell you! Even though I never meet anyone famous, I think I saw Sky Lowe at a bakery. And the way he and this woman were fighting, they are definitely a couple, so he can't be married to Natasha. Married men don't meet their mistresses in bakeries, that much I know," I said.

"Are you sure?" she asked, breathlessly.

"I'm like 95% confident that it was Sky Lowe, and 99% confident that whoever I saw is single. But I can tell Natasha likes you and that's like 100%. She even worries about you, like how you're not serious enough."

Jessica gave me a big hug, thanked me about a dozen times, and proceeded to sing the virtues of Natasha for over an hour, until she had run out of virtues to rhapsodize about. But then she said, "That still leaves you and the problem of Francois Morel."

"There is no problem of me and Francois Morel," I said.

Of course, as soon as I said that, I bumped into Francois— well, the next day, but almost as soon. He stopped and said, "You're always rushing, Bella."

I wished that I were wearing something more alluring, like my silky scarf with blue lilies. "I'm trying to get everything clear for the winter break, so I can slow down when I'm in New York."

"For your boyfriend in New York," he said. "And he, he slows down for you, too?"

"Hmm, he's very athletic," I replied. "You know, basketball, tennis, running. He's very active."

Francois took this in. "I see…and you? Are you active too?"

I realized that he was earnest. "Not in a physical sense," I said. "You see, I am bad at sports, even Ping-Pong, because I lack what people call right-left coordination. Plus, sports are impossible to understand, like why something is a strike or why it's not, and why they're always taking time out in football, and what are all those bowls? It's complicated, I think."

"Perhaps," he said, repressing the start of a smile. "Maybe you will find opera a little easier to…grasp. I gave you my favorite version—it's balanced as Mozart should be, not too fast."

"But it has feeling, not just balance. I mean, the feelings are balanced, the light, the dark, the funny, and the serious. Interpretation isn't only about tempo…anyway, thank you again…Professor Morel," I said, although I never called Natasha Lowenstein anything but Natasha. Still, it was customary to use the title.

He looked straight into my eyes and said, "Francois, I hope."

# NINE

By the time that the performance came along, I was happily humming *Figaro*'s bright opening aria. Jeremy, on the other hand, knotted his tie like an innocent man about to be hanged. He was having one of his silent nights. For twenty blocks, he ignored me.

It was a clear December night, and the Met, with its chandeliers, shone brightly. The opera crowd had a fur and perfume smell. The scent of the good life—good for everyone, that is, except Jeremy. But as the second magical act drew to its conclusion, Jeremy slipped his hand into mine. And I turned to him and kissed him. If it had been a dark movie theater, we would have started messing around like lovesick teenagers.

In hindsight, that would have been an excellent choice, even if it was the Met and not a movie theater. But the audience was rising, and we followed the perfumed tide into the lobby. And there stood, of all people, Professor Natasha Lowenstein. For a second, I thought that she was standing alongside a clone—or perhaps a man surgically altered to look like her, or maybe one of those scary doppelgängers that pop up in dark fiction? But upon second glance, I saw that the masculine double was none other than the man from the bakery, otherwise known as Sky Lowe.

Natasha greeted me with no surprise. Indeed, she would not have been fazed had we met in the Arabian sands, two camels passing one another among the white dunes. She waved us over and said, "My brother, Sky. He calls himself Lowe, but he's a Lowenstein through and through."

"You have a brother!" I shouted ecstatically.

"I have two brothers, to be accurate," said Natasha, taken aback by my enthusiasm.

Naturally, I could not reveal my fears about the Natasha-Sky marriage. It would have been disloyal to Jessica Tang, and awkward, what with incest taboos and all.

Seen side by side, the family resemblance was unmistakable: dark curly hair, pale skin, hazel eyes, a hint of a smile. A sloppier version of Natasha, with a more jovial brand of friendliness.

Sky recognized me as well, after a brief double-take. "We have to stop meeting like this." He added to Natasha, "We met at Greengrass's. Amy and I were having a bad day."

"Amy survived to eat another black-and-white," said Natasha, casting Amy into the sea of difficult girlfriends. Then she turned to Jeremy. "You must be Bella's Jeremy. Are you an opera fan?"

"No, but she won a contest, so why not?" was Jeremy's reply.

Natasha had a way of shaking her head rapidly when attempting to signal "clarity," which usually meant vanquishing the army of objections to her own arguments. To my consternation, I now perceived a few quick clarifying shakes.

She regarded me with a smirk. "Did you invent a contest? Shades of Count Almaviva, I think."

Her reference to the opera's snaky villain was not encouraging, but then again, I was hardly the virtuous Countess.

"I guess it was more of a gift, not really a contest. But the important thing is that the tickets were free," I said as I watched Jeremy's eyes go wide. My only hope was that Natasha would avoid mentioning Francois.

I searched the room, vainly hoping for inspiration. Surely some poet had a line for such moments as this. But all that sprung to mind was, "Beware of Greeks bearing gifts." That did not exactly fit the situation, except for the "beware" part, which was best left alone. In fact, the less said about "beware," the better. As for foreigners, as Elaine of Elaine's Bridal said, you never can tell.

Then I heard Sky Lowe's voice: "A gift feels like winning a contest because you feel lucky."

I wondered where the cookie-less Amy was tonight and if Natasha was her last-minute replacement. But I put sullen Amy out of my mind. It was critical to fill the air with talk, rather than allow Natasha to supply other, more lethal, ammunition.

"Exactly! It felt like winning a contest, although if you want to be strictly literal, I suppose that it was not technically a contest or even a contest at all. It was more of a random event, something improbable and unexpected, which is like a contest, in a way, since winning a contest is purely random—although, I guess, entering the contest in the first place isn't random, I suppose, since that's a matter of free will…"

I took a breather and observed Jeremy, Natasha, and Sky, whose faces bore a variety of expressions. The look-alike siblings appeared to be struggling mightily not to explode into laughter. Jeremy stared downward as through his shoes contained interesting secrets. I would have been better off if I had stuck to "Beware of Greeks bearing gifts," but wasn't there something about not looking a gift-horse in the mouth?

"Enjoy the rest of the performance," said Natasha in what I thought was a too-cheery tone. Obviously, my devious Count-like behavior tickled her funny bone, although it might have been my sheer ineptitude that amused her. Either way, I had proved entertaining, although not to Jeremy.

Sky added, "It has a happy ending. That's the good part about comic operas. Everyone ends up happy, and all's forgiven. In most opera, everyone's dead and singing about it."

The siblings laughed together, in geeky solidarity.

The gong sounded, and the intermission was, mercifully, over.

If there were no such thing as sex, which, perhaps, there will not be in the distant future, the evening might have turned grim. As it was, Mozart had inspired other thoughts. After the opera, instead of fighting, Jeremy peeled off all my layers until there was nothing left to peel and made me forget everything.

But when we were quiet, I said, "Jeremy, I know it looks bad, but I can explain."

"What? Another theory of probability? Another imaginary contest? Or another coincidental meeting with Sky Lowe? Who just happens to show up at the Met?"

"You don't think that Sky Lowe and I...? That's crazy," I asked, with a mix of incredulity and relief.

"You have a brother!" mimicked Jeremy. His impression of me wasn't half bad, either.

It was easy to reconstruct his version of the plot: a pretend bakery tryst, the gift of opera tickets, the invented contest to mask whatever the bakery tryst was supposed to, and then, my false mirth at seeing Sky at the Met. His instincts were on the mark, but he had inserted the wrong man in the picture.

"I knew that you wouldn't see an opera, so I made up the contest to make it exciting. It was Sue's idea."

"Oh," said Jeremy.

"The point is, there's nothing between me and Sky Lowe," I said—that part, at least, was completely true.

# TEN

The first day of Francois Morel's seminar "Mind, Brain, and Language" was tense. About twenty students from battling disciplines eyed one other warily. The pecking order was all too clear: the lordly neuroscientists, the serf-like social scientists, the beleaguered education students, and, from the distant humanities, the rebel scholars.

Under the circumstances, I had to admire Francois's good humor. He was serious and treated all with equal seriousness. He presented ideas as works in progress, open to challenge. "I might be wrong…" he said, almost reticently. Yet with his careful, measured reasoning, I felt that he rarely was.

After class, he approached me. He wore one of those voluminous scarves that only European men can wear without looking foppish. He watched as I donned a puffy down jacket, orange mittens, and matching orange earmuffs.

"You look very…bright today," he said, at a loss for a more flattering adjective. A man like Francois—and only a man like him—could manage to find a compliment for such a ghastly outfit.

"I am very colorful," I agreed as I adjusted my orange earmuffs and headed out.

I realized that he was escorting me outside of the building and, despite the icy January air, wore only his huge scarf and sweater. "I got your thank-you note, but it wasn't a review," he said. "You promised a review."

"I don't know enough about opera to write a review. I'd sound stupid." I wisely did not mention the dozen or more drafts that I had torn up before writing, "Thank you for the tickets, B."

"I doubt that," he said. "Anyway, I am glad you're taking my seminar."

"Natasha talked me into it. You know how she is."

"Well, she can wear anyone out," he said.

"I'd say that Natasha wins people over more than she wears them out. She usually has a good reason, even if she doesn't share it," I said.

"In this case, she does. We have a large study going on. There's funding for an interdisciplinary team, but that's easier said than done." His hangdog expression was almost comical.

I smiled. "I never thought the subject of grammar could get so, um, agitated. But you manage very well."

"I've had practice," he said. "Everyone's looking to attack, rather than to collaborate. It's hard to put together a true team. That is why Natasha suggested you."

"I'm flattered, but I am only getting started in the program," I told him. "I don't know if I'm the right person to help you. Why me?"

"Natasha passed along one of your papers on vocabulary. It had a lot of common sense. It was moderate."

"Is common sense so hard to find?" I asked.

"Surprisingly, yes," he said. "You've written about empathy and how words influence the ability to understand people. I've been studying it the other way around, but it could work both ways, no?"

"Well, the more words, the more complex the feelings—nice, kind, loyal, generous—they're different. Maybe if you lack that variety of words, you fail to discriminate. As you acquire more words, you begin to see finer differences. We could test that…but aren't you freezing out here? You're only wearing a sweater."

He rubbed his gloveless hands together as if he were first aware of the cold. "I'm fine," he said.

"You're sure?" I asked, from the comfort of my orange down.

"I am very sure," he said. "This is a time commitment. I know you have your… weekends, and this could spill over. I want you to feel comfortable."

"Jeremy, he's my boyfriend, he'll adjust. So, I feel…comfortable," I said. "I guess you need a proposal, too."

"A formality. All you need to do is take your paper and add a section on testing," said Francois. We both knew that the rule of academia was cut and paste. Any paper, properly re-jiggered, could become ten in a heartbeat.

We shook hands on it, mine gloved, his not.

As I walked away from him, I took stock. My heart was not fluttering or pitter-pattering or anything like that. With Jeremy, I was forever betwixt and between, second-guessing each word—interpreting his every glance like a Boyfriend Morse Code. I was always on edge, on the verge, in the clouds. It wasn't Jeremy's fault, but I spent hours trying to read his elusive moods or moods that seemed to me elusive until they were passionate.

Here was a man who, by contrast, was an open book. Comfortable, I repeated to myself. I feel comfortable. A new word applied to me. Francois liked to put people at ease. It was second nature to him. And maybe because he was just shy of Jeremy's kind of handsome, I felt less awkward. Even in my puffy down jacket, I felt glamorous—no easy trick, that.

I dashed off the proposal the next day. After struggling with so many versions of thank-you notes, it seemed like mere child's play. What a relief to type "Professor Morel," instead of struggling with "Francois" versus "Dear Francois" versus "F."

# ELEVEN

"The light's great," Jessica said, picking up a stray dust ball from my living room floor. "And it's quiet, too."

I had found a rental in an elegant restored Victorian brownstone: rose- and blue-colored stained-glass windows on each floor, an ornate winding staircase, freshly painted walls, gleaming hardwood floors, and an airy foyer straight out of *Architectural Digest*. Compared to my nondescript studio in Manhattan, it felt palatial—a real living room, a large bedroom overlooking a quiet street.

"I have tables and real chairs and a sofa and a desk. That's a big step up from Jeremy's place. He just has plastic stuff."

She frowned. "Right," she said.

She rummaged through the apartment, then my closets, until she discovered a few Art Deco prints and flowered rugs. "These are fabulous. Why are you hiding them?"

"I was waiting for a good excuse to take them out," I replied.

Jessica blinked a few times and jerked her head rapidly. She was starting to copy Natasha's quirks even down to these gestural tics. "You have a good excuse," she said.

"Am I giving a party?" I asked pleasantly. "What's my excuse?"

"You live here. This is what people do when they occupy their own apartments. They hang pictures. They put vases on tables and flowers in vases. They put rugs on floors, they don't store them in closets. It's called dwelling, inhabiting, *living*. You've heard about that concept, right—living?"

"Huh, interesting," I said.

As we hung the pictures, Jessica's insight telegraphed itself to me. Pictures, vases, tablecloths—they inhabited a world apart from Jeremy's and mine. We lived like two nomads in two different tents with big bookshelves. And for the life of me, I didn't know why.

"Well, it's like this. Jeremy and I have formed some habits that are hard to break. Like for instance, he doesn't own any real chairs. So we don't cook because there's no place to sit, plus he doesn't have pots or pans or a toaster or a coffeemaker. So, obviously, we can't invite anyone over. I guess we don't have much of a lifestyle. You might say that we lack a lifestyle in the true sense of 'lifestyle,'" I concluded.

"We're not talking about Jeremy," said Jessica.

I admired the walls with their new visual interest. "Pictures make a big difference. I can see why people hang them."

Jessica was not one to be deterred. "We're talking about you. You live here, Bella. Jeremy doesn't. He lives in New York by himself, in another apartment."

"Now you sound like my mother," I said.

"Fine with me," Jessica said. "Listen, let's try a real-time experiment. We'll cook dinner here like it's your real apartment and you have a guest, me. Let's see what you have for starters."

She opened my refrigerator, which, while spotless, contained only low-fat milk and some moisturizers and cosmetics. She said dolefully, "A moisturizer is not food."

"Well it's organic," I said, growing impatient. Surely my moisturizers, which had cost a small fortune, implied something like a lifestyle. But I had to concede that my pantry, so to speak, was suited for the Eating Less Diet and not the other kinds.

So that was the catalyst for my first "real" food shopping in the City of Brotherly Love. I first suggested a nearby store with a name like 23rd Street Grocery, only a half black away. But Jessica tossed off my suggestion, and instead, forced me to walk ten long blocks, which, on a chilly afternoon, took forever.

"What's wrong with the other one?" I asked.

"It wasn't a real market," Jessica said mysteriously.

We entered a store that appeared to have most of Philadelphia shopping in it—the young black-leather-jacketed men, their older tweedy counterparts, impossibly fashionable children, and their overly-attentive parents. Apparently, this qualified as a "real" market.

An elderly woman held up a pineapple and said in a loud voice, "Sometimes the pineapple is not very sweet, is it?" She seemed troubled by the large prickly fruit.

I said, "I heard that they have enzymes in them that are very beneficial for something, maybe your digestion. I think they sell them in pills. Then, you don't have to worry whether the pills are sweet or not, do you?"

"Nothing wrong with my digestion," she snapped as though I had maligned her internal systems.

"But if there ever is, you could buy a pineapple pill, which is convenient. But I'm not sure that they sell them here. Maybe you have to go to a vitamin store."

Jessica said, "I think that the pineapple is a very risky purchase, personally."

"Do you?" asked a familiar voice.

There stood Natasha Lowenstein, with an enormous Great Dane and her usual contented expression. She had a habit of showing up everywhere, without seeming the least bit surprised. Only Natasha could manage to get her huge dog into a fancy food store. No doubt, she arranged seats for him on airplanes and trains.

"I bought a pineapple the other day here, it was excellent," she advised the elderly woman.

The senior, like everyone else on the planet, accepted Natasha's expertise as a given. She happily dumped the pineapple into her cart and glared at Jessica and me.

"We meet again," I said to Natasha. "It's a good thing, too. That woman had her heart set on a pineapple. We weren't much help."

"I've had bad luck with pineapples," Jessica insisted.

Natasha smiled at Jessica. "They're not a foolproof fruit, for sure. They can be tricky."

Jessica nodded. "Exactly, that's what I meant. Anyway, we're here to shop for Bella. Her refrigerator is a disaster. It's empty, scary almost."

"But it's clean, it's not the other kind of disaster," I let Natasha know, in case she got the wrong idea. Although, from the way she was gazing at Jessica, I surmised that refrigerators were far from her thoughts. I wondered if Jessica had hoped to catch Natasha in this food emporium. Jessica did seem very well dressed, for Jessica, that is.

Perhaps Natasha got the same newsflash. She said, "I'm having some people over for dinner, so why don't you join us? I'm thinking paella. What do you think, Jessica?"

Jessica flushed, and for a terrible second, I feared that she might swoon with delight. But to her credit, she dived right in. "That's always a perfect party dish. It's easy to serve. Are you thinking chicken paella with sausage?"

The two of them entered into a lively paella debate, most of which escaped me since I had never prepared chicken, sausage, or rice, ditto saffron. But even if the ingredients were new to me, their happy exchange was anything but: Natasha had lost her edge and Jessica her hopelessness. The two chefs whizzed through the store, selecting all manner of foodstuffs with a speed that astonished the poor Great Dane.

"I hope you're paying attention. This is Chinese parsley, or cilantro, and this is Italian parsley. People always mix them up," Jessica informed me. She held them under my nose, so I could smell the difference.

Natasha laughed. "Bella's a quick study. We don't have to worry about her."

"No, you don't," I said, although I had filled my cart with fancy English teas, exotic marmalades, and little else in the way of food. "Anyway, who's coming tonight, apart from Jessica and me? Anyone we know?"

"Oh my brother, a few others from the department…and Francois Morel."

At least that gave me a reason to dress.


Natasha's apartment was like Natasha—attractive without a hint of flash, with an academic style: Navajo pottery, Persian rugs, Mission furniture, a few oil paintings, books everywhere, spilling onto coffee tables.

I made my way to where the wine was. Leaning against Sky Lowe was a gypsy-like woman, whose blue-black hair swept against him. She wore a diaphanous blue dress that almost, but not quite, fell off her shoulders. She was exquisite.

Sky said sheepishly, "Bella, meet Tatiana Biro. She's…married to Francois Morel."

She was not at all what I expected.

"I'm enrolled in 'Mind, Brain, and Language' this semester, with your husband, Professor Morel." Of course, I realized that she must know her own husband's name. Still, it couldn't hurt to offer her and Sky a reminder—the way Sky looked, he needed one and fast.

"Yes, his favorite seminar," she said in an accent that might have been Russian or Greek. She fingered the sleeve of my dress as if she were in a boutique, contemplating a purchase. "This is nice— vintage, right?"

"Thanks, I like vintage, but I can't say that my boyfriend likes it," I said and added proudly, "He lives in New York."

"My first husband was from New York," she said with the air of husbands to come. "He designed elevators. It was very stressful. He never knew when one could crash."

She lit a cigarette, or rather, Sky lit it for her. I was fascinated by her ability to hold a cigarette and wine glass in one hand, without spilling or burning anyone.

"New York's a good city if you're into elevators. I mean, it has lots of tall buildings. But maybe it wasn't the best career for him since he was so nervous," I said.

She puffed her cigarette and said in a doomed voice, "A brilliant man, very brilliant." She stared upward as though contemplating rising elevators—although maybe she was avoiding the cigarette smoke, wafting in my direction.

I asked Sky, "Are you shooting your next film in Philly?"

"I wish. I'm going crazy looking for the right material. I want to do something really scary," he answered as he fumbled to find his own cigarette. I was stuck with two smokers—but a thought had popped into my head.

Before I had to chance to pursue it, Tatiana asked in a gloomy manner, "How did the two of you meet?"

Sky started laughing to himself, and then said, "That was funny."

I said, "Not that funny."

Francois appeared to refill Tatiana's wine—beating Sky to the punch, although I doubt that was his intention. He said, pleasantly, "What is funny?"

I poked Sky, but he went on laughing helplessly. "I met Bella at the Met. She drummed up this totally weird story about having won a contest for the tickets, and then she had to get out of it, ha ha. I couldn't figure out why she made up the contest."

I shrugged and sipped the wine that was fast delivering a headache. Or was it Tatiana's musky perfume that was so nauseating?

Tatiana smiled a cat's smile. "A man gave her the tickets, Sky. Why else would she invent such a story? Really, sometimes men are idiots."

Sky stopped laughing. "Oh," he said, looking miserable.

By now, the smoke was making my eyes water. I wiped them and made some blurry excuses about allergies and needing aspirin—and then I found a smokeless hallway. Exhaling, I leaned against the wall. A few seconds later, Francois followed—and looked at me with his plain, serious eyes.

"She was teasing you, it's nothing," he said.

I tried to steady my voice, in case it gave me away. "It sounds ridiculous about the opera, but Jeremy gets jealous."

"He's in love, why not?" Francois asked. The way he put it, it did sound pretty normal.

"Believe it or not, he was worried about me and Sky Lowe. And you're not worried, I guess, about your wife and…"

"No, I'm not…bothered. Can you understand?" he asked gently.

"Probably not, it's too European for me," I admitted. "She's going to break his heart. Your wife is very beautiful."

He laughed and said, "You're melodramatic."

"I'm American," I said, on the defensive.

Francois waved in the direction of where Sky stood. "And he's ambitious, and so is she. These kinds of affairs, they burn out. And why does it concern you?"

"I worry about everyone, to tell you the truth. But you're right—it's none of my business. I'm just annoyed at myself. I lied for no reason. And it wasn't just about jealousy, it's hard to explain."

"Please, you don't need to explain. Tell me about the opera instead," he said. "Don't worry about what you know and don't know."

"Well, I love how the songs are serious and funny at the same time and even though the story is all a joke, the music says it isn't. I loved how all the voices blend together, but always in different ways, just the way people and relationships change. And I almost cried for the Countess, the way she sang it, I could hear all the disappointment." I stopped myself before I choked up. "Anyway, that's my review, Professor Morel."

He smiled at me, for a long time, or that is how it felt—and I suppose that I was smiling, too. "I think Jeremy's right to be jealous," he said.

But that wasn't the end of the evening.

# TWELVE

I took a gamble. As the party was winding down, I caught Sky. "I have a bee in my bonnet," I told him, "So please meet with me tomorrow? Say yes, you won't be sorry."

He smiled at the old-fashioned-ness of my request. And he said, "Of course," as if we already were the best of buddies. I imagined that in the movie business, friends were more or less a fleeting thing anyway.

We met at a small neighborhood bar near Fitler Square. Sky arrived late, but not so late that it mattered—pleasantly rumpled in a flannel shirt and jeans that had seen better days. And without bothering about vintage, he ordered a bottle of wine and poured us rather large glasses, filled to the rim.

Sky plunged into a history of his affair with Tatiana—maybe he figured that I was curious, which, it so happened, I was. He didn't have much to tell, but he made the most of it: the first meeting, the first blush, the inevitable confession, and so on. He concluded, sighing, "I'm depressed. I mean it's like *Double Indemnity* and I'm Fred McMurray."

Listening to Sky, I felt that his wasn't a bad sort of gloom, involving a good deal of crowded bars and loud music, and little of staring hopelessly into open spaces. In fact, it was fair to say that Sky's depressed was livelier than Jeremy's happy. He enjoyed making a fool of himself over a gorgeous woman, and I suspected that Tatiana was the latest in a series of unattainables.

I said, "Fred McMurray is a seriously underrated actor."

"Fred's great. I love Fred," Sky said refilling our glasses. "Listen, I'm sorry if I embarrassed you at the party."

"Forget it," I said. "Let's talk about your film, or what is going to be your next film when you stop being depressed. That's what I want to talk about."

"I guess you're writing a screenplay," he said, in a resigned voice.

"Never," I replied.

"Whew, that's a relief. It's like a disease, these screenplays," he said.

"Maybe you need a vaccine," I said. "I'll make you a pledge. I promise never ever to write a screenplay, not even a film noir. Even if you begged me right now on bended knees, I wouldn't say yes."

"I'll drink to that," he said, swilling more wine. "But don't repeat what I said about writing screenplays, because Tatiana's writing one."

"About?"

Sky thought about it. "Some poet. He gets shot by a firing squad, which is cool, but, you see, he's Bulgarian. I try to tell her, find a Russian or a Pole or someone from a big country. There just aren't that many Bulgarians."

"Or poets," I observed.

"Right," he agreed, pouring more.

"Anyway, I didn't call you about a screenplay. My boyfriend Jeremy, you met him at the opera, he writes stories, he's very talented. They're called *Scared Jim* stories. I think you need to read them."

"*Scared Jim*, that's a cool title," said Sky, happily. "Cool title."

"Exactly," I said. "And the stories are seriously cool. Scared Jim falls into other people's nightmares, like he falls into the bottom of a well, he falls into car accidents. You said you wanted scary. These are, believe me."

"Short stories are tough to work with. They don't have an arc, you know what I mean?"

"So? Lots of projects start with something hard. Like *Casablanca*, which no one expected to be a hit. You know, it was based on a play that never even got published, called *Everybody Comes to Rick's*."

"That's a bad title, *Everybody Comes to Rick's*," he said as he refilled our glasses.

"Terrible title." It might have been the wine, but terrible title sounded like a tongue twister. I tried it again but more slowly, "Terrible title, terrible title, terrible title."

"*Scared Jim*, cool title," he said.

"Exactly, it's a cool title. And, you know, this wine isn't giving me a headache. You and Natasha know about wine. I should write down the name, but I don't have a pen or even paper."

Sky began to write the name of the wine on a napkin and said, "I'm not going to ask if Jeremy knows that we are talking about this."

"Since you're not going to ask, I'm not going to answer. My apartment is only a block or two from here. I can give you the stories. Read them for yourself."

"Bella, this seems not such a great idea if you haven't talked about it with Jeremy."

I downed another glass of the excellent wine with speed. "Yet, not yet," I said. "That's a minor detail, in my opinion."

"Not that minor, actually kind of major."

"Minor or major, it shouldn't stop you. You might as well know that I am stubborn."

"No kidding," he laughed. "You don't give up, do you?"

"No, not really," I said. "I think it's a genetic thing, being stubborn. If you think about it, no one learns how to be stubborn. Personally, I prefer the word patient, which everyone says is a virtue like a saint. No one says, 'Isn't that great, she's really stubborn!'"

"In Hollywood, they do. Producers need to be stubborn," Sky said thoughtfully.

"Then pretend that I'm a movie producer. The two of you can thank me at the Oscars because, believe me, you will win an Oscar. Well, Jeremy probably won't come to the Oscars because he hates to fly, and he doesn't do drugs or alcohol, so he'd feel out of it."

"No flying, no drinking, I guess he's…" said Sky.

"Creative," I replied sadly.

By the time we left the bar, it was later than I'd planned. Plus, it was raining, not a downpour, but enough to streak my eyeliner and flatten whatever remained of my so-called hairstyle. Happily, Sky looked worse—matted long hair, his shirt hanging out. I didn't care if my apartment was a mess. Sky would hardly notice one way or the other.

But we did notice that the lights were on. "Hmm," I said as I opened the door. "That's definitely weird."

Another evening, it might have been weird. But as fate would have it, it was not weird at all, given that Jeremy was seated inside, book in hand. He took in the unwelcome presence of a damp Sky Lowe and me, standing unsteadily after consuming the better part of a bottle of wine, or was it two.

"Jeremy, you're early," I informed him, to which he gave a skeptical nod—since, in point of fact, he was on time and I was late. "You remember Sky Lowe, um, Natasha Lowenstein's brother."

"I do," said Jeremy with a hostile glare.

Sky looked around, perplexed. "Hey, I don't hear music. And you're reading," he said to Jeremy.

Jeremy, tight-jawed, held up a book. It was his one of his idols, a South American poet who wrote of prisons and suicides. The sight of Sky, as I knew, was enough to put Jeremy in a foul mood, and that grim poetry might push him over the edge.

"Yes, I am reading," he said.

"You know, I can never read without music," Sky said, chattily. "For me personally, it's critical for me to calibrate every single book to music. That's a basic part of the whole reading experience. But you know, it's funny, I never need words to listen to music. I never hear a song and think, wait, I need a book. Kind of strange, isn't it?"

"Maybe because the songs have words in them, you know, song lyrics," I pointed out. It might have been the wine, but my insight struck me as brilliant. I briefly entertained the notion of writing a paper on it.

"Very astute," Jeremy said. "Songs have words. It's the whole song experience."

Put that way, my idea seemed less intriguing, in fact downright dull. Music would have come in handy at a time like this—something upbeat, with a carefree bouncy lyric, like "Happy Days Are Here Again" or, come to think of it, "Singin' in the Rain."

Sky broke the silence. "Bella asked me to read your stories, which she says are scary, and I like the title *Scared Jim*—it's a cool title."

From his messenger bag, he produced a bunch of folders—I guess that he used them for notes. And he eased his soggy form into one of the chairs, making himself at home, dripping everywhere. It would have been rude to advise him against it, though, even if I wanted to—at least he wasn't smoking.

Jeremy looked down at his loafers—and I had to admit, he looked his best when sulking or brooding. "Don't you live in New York, Sky?" he asked.

I said, "His girlfriend lives in Philly."

"Tatiana is not exactly my girlfriend," added Sky, somewhat unhelpfully.

Jeremy nodded in a scholarly fashion. "She's not."

"She is almost a girlfriend. In fact, she is Sky's girlfriend for all practical intents and purposes," I said.

"Interesting," Jeremy said.

To drive home the point, I added, "And she is very, very beautiful," although it was unclear why Tatiana's beauty rendered her more authentic, girlfriend-wise.

I opened the cabinet and produced a lone box of water wafers from London. I scattered a few on a plate, which I placed in the center of the table. On a large white platter, they appeared even more unappetizing than they had in the package. This was the unhappy result of my food shopping. It seemed unlikely that such a flimsy offering would improve any man's mood, much less Jeremy's.

"So, where is she?" asked Jeremy. "The girlfriend or the almost girlfriend?"

"Well, it's complicated," I said brightly.

Sky laughed in his dopey way. "It's a real mess," he said. "She's married."

"But her husband isn't a jealous person, so it's not really a mess. He's my professor, Francois Morel, and he's not jealous about Sky. You see, they're European."

Jeremy said, "That's a relief."

Sky ignored the sarcasm, or maybe he was too drunk to notice. "So, let's have a look at the stories—*Scared Jim*, cool title. Bella kind of talked me into reading them. You know how stubborn she can be."

"Yes, our Bella is very stubborn," said Jeremy, not smiling.

"Absolutely, but that's not a bad thing," Sky said. "I mean, that's why I'm here, to read the stories."

"Without music?" asked Jeremy.

Sky looked confused until the connection hit him. "Right...without music, I get it. That's kind of funny," he said.

"But you're right. It would work better with music, like a theremin effect like in *The Day the Earth Stood Still*. Love that film."

"You know, most people think it was a theremin in *Forbidden Planet*, but it wasn't," I said. "It was actually a ring modulator, which sounds like the theremin, but isn't. A lot of people get that one wrong."

"Ring modulator, I never knew that, very cool," said Sky. He had no way of knowing that Jeremy hated slang, much less retro slang like cool or neat or swell. "So let's see these stories."

Jeremy had begun to stare at his loafers, in that way he had of inspecting footwear at critical times. "Jeremy," I said, or pleaded or wheedled or whined.

Jeremy's face was motionless. He shook his head, very slightly, no.

"Jeremy," I said, but he looked toward the wall, away from me.

There was a long, sticky silence, the kind that, I knew, could last all night or longer. Sky's eyes darted to where the *Scared Jim* stories lay on the table.

Sky said, "Hey, I get it, it's your material. If this isn't a good time—or if you're not okay sharing them."

Jeremy said, "I'm not...okay."

Sky got up. "Writers...well, I need to get going." With that, he dropped his folders and notepads and created something of a mess or, in hindsight, a distraction.

I walked him to the door and said, "Thanks for the drink and I'm sorry for wasting your time. I guess I am too stubborn sometimes."

"I wouldn't say that," said Sky.

After the door shut, I couldn't figure out whether I felt angry or frustrated or something else. "What was that about?" I asked, leaning against the door.

"I don't know where to start," he replied.

"Start with why you were rude," I said. "I'm sure Hemingway and all those guys had help. That's all I was trying to do, help you."

"That's cool," said Jeremy, mocking.

"That's the way people talk in L.A. Give it a chance, Jeremy," I said.

"A chance for me to be like Sky Lowe? Is that what I want? Or is that what you want? Or doesn't it matter?"

"You're being ridiculous. If you were successful, you wouldn't become Sky Lowe. You'd still be you, only with more choices. You could do what you like. We would have more choices, you and I."

"This was my choice. That's what this is about. I haven't published these yet."

"Jeremy, it's also about us. It's not just your life, or at least that's not how I see it. We don't have parents with money and that's OK—it is fine. But that means that we have to figure this out ourselves. What's wrong with a shortcut?"

"You should have asked me first," he said.

"If I asked, we both know your answer. With you, it is no, it's no chairs, it's no toaster, it's no this, no that. You're like the Master of No, like it's a religion, which last time I checked, it was not. I mean, the Pope has really fantastic furniture and art and everything, and he is a very religious person. And there's nothing between me and Sky, except that he is the only film director whom I've met or probably will ever meet. And he was willing to read your stuff. So yes, we got a little drunk or more than a little drunk and so what?"

"Some guy you hardly know comes up to your apartment for no reason and you're both more than a little drunk. And you say, let's go read some stories," he said. "Please."

Jeremy seemed intent on twisting the night's events into some Hollywood plot, complete with a cigar-smoking director and a star-crazed loony, which turned out to be me of all people. "It's not like that. And it wasn't for no reason. It was for you, because I love you. You know that."

He shook his head, first in disbelief, and then in amusement. We kissed a long time, quiet kisses not the other kind. And then I said, "I'm sorry."

He whispered, "I know."

But he was wrong. I wasn't sorry, not even a little.

I'd lied for the second time to Jeremy. This time, it felt worse. The opera lie was an accident, like a train that leaves the station as you hit the platform. But this one, this lie, felt deliberate. I had hidden my feelings because I knew that he wouldn't—and couldn't—accept them. Our views were too far apart and even as I tried to picture the future with Jeremy, it seemed like a distant, forbidden planet.

The next morning was bright and cold, the sky swept clean by the rain. I'd gotten into the habit of rising early, making coffee and sifting through my piles of papers, journals, and file cards. Jeremy was in the shower. The sun was shining. A rare, lazy morning lay ahead of us. But then I noticed…something was out of place. Of course, I knew what it was.

I waited for Sky's call for what felt like hours. I picked up the receiver on the first ring, before it had died down. I needed to be careful in case Jeremy was listening.

Sky's voice was unrecognizable from the night before—fast-talking, excited, all business. He said, "OK, I stole the stories when you weren't looking. I figured you wouldn't mind since you'd left them out. You guessed that already, right?"

"Correct," I said. "And?"

"I'm blown away. Tell Jeremy I want to talk with him today, like right now. He's got to come back to L.A. with me. Now."

"Not New York?"

"Nah, this isn't some little indie film, it needs a big budget, special effects. It's an L.A. project."

"Right," I said unhappily. "But aren't you going to miss…people?"

"You can't have it both ways, Bella," Sky said.

Jeremy was drying himself as he listened to my side of the conversation. He gave me one of his shy, almost-smiles—and his eyes never looked as dark to me as they did right then. But, as Sky said, I couldn't have it both ways. I handed Jeremy the phone and stood aside as everything started happening fast, and then faster, until it got away.

# THIRTEEN

I don't know how long I had been asleep when the phone rang. "Jeremy," I said instead of hello. "What time is it?" I was in that twilight between dreaming and waking, which I always liked.

"Midnight, your time," he answered.

Of course, it was my time, not his. After months apart, I hardly needed a reminder.

It was one of those full-moon nights, bright enough to illuminate my bedroom. I don't know why, but I started to question if the Earth turned around every day, and if that was why there was a day and a night. Or was it because the Earth circled around the Sun? Half asleep, I couldn't recall.

I was about to ask when I heard Jeremy say in a sort of strangled voice, "I'm not coming back in July, so I wanted you to know."

I snuggled under the warm blanket. "Oh, July, August, whenever you come, I'm here. I wish you were here, too. I'm lonely."

There was a long, hard silence before I heard his voice again, so low that I had to strain to hear it. "It's not that simple," he murmured.

I switched the lamp on and propped myself up against the pillow. The harsh electric light was the very opposite of cool moonlight. "People always say it's not simple when they mean the opposite. It is very simple, Jeremy. Either you are coming back or you're not," I said. "I guess you've made up your mind."

"I have," he said.

"And you're not asking me. You're telling me—or is that a stupid question?"

"This is what you wanted, isn't it? You said I might get hired to write the official screenplay. I did. You said it might be a big movie, and it is. Plus, now Sky is talking about a sequel."

"Don't tell me, *More Scared Jim*," I said, momentarily distracted. "Wow, a sequel before there's even a finished screenplay. What a weird world."

"It's the way the business works," he said. "Listen, I'm not keeping my apartment in New York. I thought you'd want to move your stuff out."

That woke me up in a big way. "Your lease goes until June, and it's only March. We have time, don't we?"

"No," he said. "The building's going condo. They're willing to pay me to leave. I didn't leave much stuff behind. So, I called Hank, the super, and he's trashing it—it's junk, anyway, like you said. I got all new things for my place in Santa Monica, one of those leather sofas you like."

"You called Hank," I said, mostly to myself.

I meant: you called him before you called me. Jeremy had decided to move to L.A. permanently without asking me. He was decorating his apartment, as I nagged him to, only without me. He had bought a leather sofa, too. Jeremy, leather sofa, hard to contemplate. For all I knew, he had bought Le Creuset pans, too.

Jeremy went on, "Hank is a nice guy. So everything's going except your clothes, unless you want him to get rid of those too. They're kind of old."

Call it a bridge too far but insulting my beloved vintage dresses was too much to bear. "I hope that you're not comparing a vintage dress collection, which is irreplaceable, to yellow plastic chairs that no homeless shelter would accept. I have original Hattie Carnegies, not that you would know or care."

He sighed—a long, suffering, telephonic sigh. "I guess your gay friends like them," he said.

"Which means what?" I said, trying to stay neutral but not succeeding. The way this call was going, he might start calling me "Babe."

There was another silence, more awkward. Where had Jeremy acquired this blasé way of speaking?

"Listen, we don't need to talk about this. I love you and I don't care what you wear. It doesn't matter to me."

"Apparently it does, and not in a good way," I said.

"Look, I have a lot going on. I'm just trying to avoid problems."

The receiver felt heavy. "So now I'm a problem," I said.

I knew what I sounded like: the textbook case of the Moody, Difficult Girlfriend. I was forcing Jeremy to haggle over closets and old dresses, while he was busy creating movie monsters and solving the complexities of time travel. I wondered if, even now, as we spoke, he was poring over his latest scene—spicing up dialogue to make it hip or edgy or whatever.

"You're not a problem," he said, meaning, of course, that I was.

I wanted him to say, "Bella, fly out this weekend. I have the money, it doesn't matter. Fly out now, call a taxi. Fly out tonight, now. I need to see you." That's what I was waiting for. That is what I wanted to hear.

But instead, all he said was, "I love you. I'll call tomorrow."

And I said, "I love you." But saying it felt like a defeat—a small one, but a defeat.

I hid my head under the pillow, so that it was black. I tried to remember what the Earth was doing, spinning, or turning. If Jeremy had been with me, sex would have done its usual magic. It wasn't a panacea, but sex had a way of fooling you into believing it was—the way that nighttime makes all cities beautiful, even when they're drab and dirty by daylight. And now we were stuck with words and we weren't getting anywhere. We were bad talkers in the best of times.

Over the next month, the "issue" of the vintage dresses hung over me, like a grim thick cloud. I couldn't face telling anyone about Jeremy's L.A. move. I could anticipate the empty phrases: a new exciting phase, an opportunity for growth, and other words that plastered over the dreary reality. Worse, some friends might note that real boyfriends helped you move. They didn't skip town and leave you with the mess. My mother was right: A man shouldn't buy his own furniture. But I didn't want to hear her say it, again.

Finally, I got around to the gory details. I found an empty clean carton in the lab/basement of the Vocabulary Project—huge, too. I loaded it with a stack of computer printouts that I needed to take home. I packed them neatly but couldn't find a clip to secure them.

Still, almost perfect, I told myself, which it might have been, had I kept my balance as I hauled it up the narrow stairwell. But as it was, I landed, facedown and, naturally, squashed the box. Papers flew in every possible direction, fluttering like an academic snowstorm. And I found myself staring at Francois, or Professor Morel, as I called him in the lab. He was descending as I was ascending or attempting an ascent.

He helped me up and asked, "What are you doing?" I noticed that he wore one of his oversized sweaters, which felt reassuring, although why was hard to say.

"Hmm, good question." I pointed to the mangled object, formerly a carton and said, "I was carrying papers in this. I needed a box."

"I could give you a paper bag," he suggested in a gentle, almost frightened, fashion. Perhaps he thought me a bit unhinged to be hauling a huge box with a small pile of paper in it, although, with a wife like Tatiana, he might be used to odd behavior. At least I wasn't writing a screenplay about an obscure Bulgarian poet. He had to grant me that much.

"I can't use a paper bag. Well, I could if it were only paper that I needed to carry. But I need a large box for my dresses. They're in New York," I told him. "But obviously, now that it is all squashed, I need another box, maybe not this big, maybe a different size."

"So it's a lot for you to carry. You're just one…person." He did not add, although it was perhaps in his thoughts, that I was one very skinny person. Since Jeremy's departure, I had shrunk to a size zero and was plummeting into negative territory.

I let him in on my battle plan, or as much of the strategy as I'd developed. "I'll get a car service to 30th Street, and I can take Amtrak, which goes direct to New York. Then I can get a taxi from Penn Station. I'll need a day when it's sunny, or at least when it's not raining. So, a lot of elements have to fall into place for it to work, assuming I get a large container, which I need for my dresses because…well, Jeremy's not coming back."

"Ah, I see," said Francois in his sober, unaffected way.

"You see, the super is getting rid of Jeremy's stuff, which isn't much and is pretty horrible, except for my vintage dresses, which are special. I've collected them for years, even before college. The building's going condo and Jeremy is staying in L.A. to work on Sky's movie," I said, becoming miserable and saying more than I had intended. "There's a sequel to *Scared Jim* even before there's a movie or even a real screenplay. That's the way Hollywood works."

"Yes, my wife told me. Tatiana's out in L.A. with Sky, now," he said as if reporting the whereabouts of two casual friends, rather than his wife and her film director/lover. "You know, her screenplay, she's trying to…develop it, I think, is the word."

Now it was my turn to say, "I see."

Francois said, "You look a little dazed, Bella. You're usually so…cheerful."

It was strange to hear myself described that way. "Actually, I'm feeling sort of mixed up. The other day, I couldn't remember if the Earth turns every twenty-four hours, which is bizarre. I mean, how could I forget what causes day and night? And I forgot if the Moon circles the Earth, but I know everything's turning. Even when it seems like we're standing still, we're not, we're spinning. The universe is moving all the time. I used to know all these facts."

Francois found a stray paper I had dropped. "You know them. You're thinking about them in a new way, so they start to seem strange."

"I don't know what I know," I said.

"Look, why don't I drive you to New York on Saturday and help you pick up your beautiful dresses? We could have a nice lunch. Or we could go to a museum. We can talk about your research or we could talk about the Sun and the Moon. That's up to you."

I felt my shoulders loosen, as if a load had been lifted from them. But still, I told him, "I couldn't ask you to do that. It's not fair."

"But you're not asking me," he said. "I am asking you, Bella. Will you come with me?"

No man had ever spoken to me as simply as Francois—or looked at me so directly, without any apology or reservations. He wasn't shy or bold. He merely asked what he wanted. If he wanted more, he would ask me, I knew.

I said, "Yes, and thank you very much."

"No, it's I who must thank you," he said, handing me the rest of my papers. It was a simple gesture, his thanks, but it made me happy. He was an easy man to please.

We drove to New York a few days later. As it happened, it was a clear day with no one on the road. I had feared that Francois might be one of those fierce Europeans who drives tiny cars at breakneck speeds. But he drove a grey four-door sedan and didn't change lanes or curse at slow drivers. I leaned back to enjoy the long, calm ride.

"I don't know how to drive, but it's one of my goals," I told him. "If I ever go to L.A, I'll need to drive because no one walks out there. It's like a city of cars."

"Very American," said Francois. I wasn't sure whether he meant me or L.A. Either way, it was true.

The Upper West Side of Manhattan, early Saturday morning, was peaceful, the way it feels before a storm. Before I knew it, we were in front of Jeremy's building near Riverside Drive, windier and colder than the rest of the city. Francois had brought plastic bags, paper bags, small bags, large bags, not to mention boxes, too.

"We don't want anything to get wrinkled," he told me as we entered the elevator.

I laughed at his anxious expression, which, up to that point, I had only seen in the classroom. "I think we're prepared," I said.

The building was a dusty mess. Workers were tearing it apart, ripping up the musty carpets and floral wallpaper—no doubt to be replaced by pale hardwood and mirrors. Jeremy's apartment, without furniture, seemed even smaller and darker, and had the strong smell of ammonia. I panicked. Ugly smells like cigarette smoke and bleach sunk into delicate fabrics and were impossible to get out. The clothes might be ruined.

But I had worried about the wrong thing. My dresses were gone, every last one of them. All I found inside the narrow unlit closets was a lone basketball. The super must have saved it for his son, a sweet curly-haired kid. He probably trashed what he saw as old clothes, not worth selling. An oversight on Jeremy's part: As he had said, he had a lot on his plate. Nothing stands still, I thought—everything is moving. And I locked the door to Jeremy's apartment for one last time.

I didn't say a word to Francois since, really, what was there to say? I avoided his eyes as we returned to the city street that, now, seemed artificially bright and lively, as if it were staged—kids running around, moms with overpriced strollers. It had been a long morning. And before I noticed, Francois Morel took my hand and pressed it against him. And he led me to Hayden's Planetarium, so I could remember everything I knew about the Sun, the Moon, and the stars.

# FOURTEEN

In my mother's version of what I had come to term The Vintage Clothing Saga, a criminal gang led by Hank the Super stole 1940s garments from unsuspecting tenants and sold them to the underground vintage market, all for a pretty penny.

"Except for the whole home-repair thing, Hank was a good super," I told her. "I think he is more of a spiritual type of person, not into the material side of things."

"That's what Jeremy says," she said, all-knowing. "And if Jeremy is so forgetful, why didn't he forget when his lease was up?"

"Right, Jeremy was in on the gang. He wouldn't know a Balenciaga if it fell on him. Now he's into the black market for vintage dresses. Please."

"Trust me, there's something wrong," she said. "But it was nice of that professor to drive you to New York. What is his name again?" she asked. Since her memory bank included summer camp counselors, piano teachers, ballet teachers, not to mention every classmate from kindergarten on, her forgetfulness seemed contrived, to put it mildly.

"Professor Morel," I said reverting to the formal, to keep the record straight.

"I think that there are Jewish Morels, maybe Sephardic."

"The thing is, Mom, most people on the planet are not Jewish. That is a statistical reality that you must accept. And don't say, 'You never know,' because in this case, I do know."

"He sounds like a nice man," she said, and then noted, "I guess he's married."

I kept my answer brief and to the point in case Jeremy overheard—he was in the bedroom. "Correct, and it's not my business."

"Where was the wife when he was driving you on a Saturday?" was her next question. My mother's psychic antennae probed in all the right places or the wrong ones, depending on your perspective. Before I lost a pound, she bought me a smaller-sized dress—and ditto, if I gained one. She was always a step ahead.

"She was out of town on…business. She is developing a screenplay with Sky Lowe, the director who's doing Jeremy's movie. The *Kill More or Die!* guy."

"Who watches such garbage about people killing and dying? Tell Jeremy these movies are made for morons," she said.

"Don't worry. Her script is about some Bulgarian poet who was either a revolutionary or he fought the revolution. Either way, he ended up being shot."

"Oh, Nikola Vaptsarov," she said as if speaking of an old, dear school chum. "Yes, the Communists killed him. He was a brilliant man, very handsome. You should be reading books like that, serious books…and wasn't Sky Lowe Natasha Lowenstein's brother? Crazy world."

Surely no odder than her knowledge of the tragic poet, I thought, but best to let it go before she shipped me a boatload of Bulgarian poetry.

"Academia is kind of like a big dysfunctional family where everyone knows everyone else, and they fight all the time and then they eat. Besides, why shouldn't Natasha have a brother?"

"Poor man," she mused, almost dreamily.

By now, I was lost. "Sky Lowe? Or the Bulgarian poet?"

"No, your nice professor—that doesn't sound like a very happy marriage," she said before she hung up.

I crawled back into bed with Jeremy, where we had spent the weekend fooling around. I hadn't seen him in months, which he blamed on the craziness of Hollywood, and I blamed on him. But the fooling around part was the same, even better if possible. It's true what they say about absence.

I had two small deco tables on either side of my bed. On the side where Jeremy slept were my beloved P.G. Wodehouse novels, to which I had added Jeremy's favorites, Beckett's trilogy, Flann O'Brien's *At Swim-Two-Birds*, and Cavafy poems in two translations. But Jeremy reached across and grabbed one of the thick tomes on my side—there was a stack of them, with forbidding titles like *Foundations of Ethnolinguistics, Sociolinguistics and Language Practice*, and so on.

In a stern voice, I said, "Please, these are not books that people read. These are books that are assigned because, well, they're…"

"The price of a graduate education," he said calmly as he took it from me. He nodded, mock-professorially, as he read the blurb. "An invaluable resource for analyzing discourse," he recited. He went on deadpan, "Let's see. Hmm, Table of Contents, Ethnography of Speaking, The Structure of Conversations, Politeness and Politeness Formulas, Terms of Address, Language and Power. Sounds gripping."

I wrested the book back from him and haughtily carried the rest of the pile over to my desk—and Jeremy followed me, hands around my waist. It was hard to look dignified since I was wearing a ridiculously sheer negligée that he had bought me, in baby blue of all colors. Trust Jeremy to go for pastels.

He said, "I think language and power is pretty hot stuff out in L.A., too."

"It might be, but I can't drive," I said. "I am a walking person."

He kissed the nape of my neck. "That's why they have driving schools."

"I don't want to be trapped in a big machine in which, at any moment, someone can kill you because they're always in a hurry, and why are they speeding? Where are they going that's so important? The only thing that I'd like about driving is being in a traffic jam and having nothing to do except listen to music."

"Go to UCLA. Westwood has sidewalks. You can walk to class. And the rest of the time, we can sit in traffic and do…nothing." He ran his hands over my hipbones to suggest the kind of nothing he had in mind and spun me around.

"I'm working on a big study. I can't just leave," I said. "I made a commitment."

"To the study," Jeremy said cautiously. He gave me a cloudy stare. And I returned one equally blank and tried not to think of Francois and his oversized sweaters.

The next day, Jeremy decided to attend Francois's "Advanced: Mind, Brain, and Language" with me. He said that he felt "curious," which was, in itself, curious. "You're going to be bored," I told him.

"No, I won't," Jeremy said.

In its third term, the seminar group, which had begun in acrimony, was relaxed and almost jolly. Intellectual disputes persisted, but the debates were, like Francois himself, calm and good-natured. Francois had collected our anecdotes of experiments gone awry, data gone missing, and many misguided theories disproved. Even Jeremy laughed.

Afterwards, Francois came over to us. It was the first time that I had seen the two of them together: Jeremy in his preppy button-down, Francois in his Euro-style turtleneck. Standing next to Francois, Jeremy seemed boyish and unfinished. I'd never thought of Jeremy as young since he was older than I by a few years. But that made him all of twenty-eight. Anyway, Francois had a sophistication that came naturally, at least to French people. We ran though the usual intros: meaningless patter about plane flights, weather, both sunny and rainy, mutual acquaintances of Sky Lowe and Tatiana, the merits of L.A. vs. New York.

Then Jeremy added, tactlessly, "Tatiana's boasted about what a good teacher you are, I mean, to Sky and me. You really are."

My first thought was, what kind of bizarre woman praises her husband to her lover? But Francois seemed pleased. "It's one of the many privileges of marriage. Your wife can praise you all she likes," he observed as if speaking of the little faithful woman. "I know that Tatiana admires your writing. She's mentioned how talented you are."

I hid my irritation at this fan club of Tatiana's—first her own husband, now Jeremy, who next? Well, I was not about to be outdone by her in the boasting department!

"Jeremy is a brilliant writer," I gushed. "His *Scared Jim* stories are really scary. They will make a great movie, and there's going to be a sequel." I smiled at them brightly.

"It's Sky's movie. I'm just a screenwriter. That's not really a writer," Jeremy replied, as if "just a screenwriter" was no big deal, as if every writer in Manhattan and L.A. wasn't dying for his job. He managed to make it pedestrian and even pathetic, as though he were an underpaid hired hand.

Francois was accustomed to soothing the anxieties of grad students. He said, "I doubt that. Sky Lowe obviously picked you because of your talent. There's no shortage of writers in L.A. or anywhere else, is there?"

I suppose that, after all of my gushing, I expected a quid pro quo. This was Jeremy's big chance to confess that it wasn't his oversized genius that landed him a Hollywood stint. No, his faithful girlfriend (i.e., me) had put herself on a limb with Sky Lowe, while the clueless boyfriend (i.e., Jeremy) hadn't lifted a pinky. If Jeremy aimed for comic effect, he could stress how he'd fought me tooth and nail and then leapt at the first chance to fly off to Hollywood. Or he could weave a humble tale concluding with a line about owing it all to his plucky, devoted—well, me! Really, he had many narrative modes, if you will, at his disposal.

Any words would do the trick, so long as they ended with a "Thank you, Bella."

Then I heard Jeremy saying, sardonically, "I was just lucky. Hollywood is all about luck." He smirked, as if enjoying a secret insider joke, and since I didn't find it funny, it was insider in the extreme.

Francois said with his mild tolerance, "Ah, you're being modest."

I recalled some quote, which goes something like: The only sure thing about luck is that it is sure to change. But I kept it to myself—the ups and downs of the film business being a cliché, not to mention the vagaries of the path of true love. And for lack of anywhere better, I looked out the window at what passed for a view. It was a defiantly hideous post-modern concrete structure, the kind that was popping up all over Philadelphia.

"It's kind of sad, isn't? This is the ugliest building ever and some poor architect designed it. He probably worked on it for years and was all excited about it. Poor man," I said and then stopped myself. I was starting to sound like my mother, never a good thing in public.

Jeremy laughed. "Bella always worries about everyone."

Francois said, "That's not such a bad quality, I think."

"Well, it does look like a jail, like a big cement jail. It's pathetic," I said.

"Believe it or not, that particular architect won a national award for excellence in design for that. I'm the one you should pity. I'm forced to look at it every day. Actually, you'll have to look at it too, for the next few years," said Francois. He smiled at me, as if grateful for the fact of me, as if he counted on it.

"I think we'll survive," I said, returning his smile.

Jeremy and I walked quietly back to Center City. The route took us over one of the bridges that cross the Schuylkill River. Over a dozen bridges crossed the river, each with its own hidden story, its own personality—to me, it was one of the pleasures of living in Philadelphia. We stopped to admire the sailboats gliding over the water, and the reflections of the arches in the glassy-blue river. I never tired of the view.

I said, "You're not going to believe this. My mother thinks that Hank stole the clothes and made a fortune selling off the Hattie Carnegies, and you were in on the plot. It's insane, but you know her. She thinks there was some kind of vintage clothing gang."

He emitted a nervous sound that bordered on a chuckle. "It wasn't really a gang," he said, and then repeated his ghastly imitation of a laugh. "But she's not entirely off-base, which is kind of funny."

"This would be funny if it were funny," I said. "If, for example, you weren't you, and I wasn't me, like if we were two totally different people. Then maybe I'd get the joke."

"Bella, no one planned this. It's just that Hank met this woman, Arlene. She's an actress and he was kind of crazy about her. Anyway, he says that they were a perfect fit."

"The clothes and Arlene were a perfect fit, or Hank and Arlene were?"

"The clothes," he said.

"Oh, my clothes, you mean, the ones that belonged to me. They were a perfect fit for some woman named Arlene who is an actress. That is really too sweet, very touching."

"Well, they were way too baggy for you. They didn't fit you anymore, they were hanging on you. I mean, look at you." He made another grating sound that might have passed for laughter.

My head had begun to throb, as it does before a migraine. I let out a big breath, puffing out my cheeks as I exhaled. Slowly, I told myself, take it slowly. Breathe in, breathe out. Relax.

"So, let me get this straight. Hank and a woman named Arlene took my clothes, which just happen to look better on her, and they lived happily ever after, not counting whatever spiritual qualms they had about…well, stealing things that didn't belong to them in the first place. And you couldn't get my clothes back or you didn't try to. Is that the gist of the story?"

"Not exactly. You see, Arlene went missing in action. Hank says lots of apartments in the neighborhood are going condo, so…I guess there are a lot of other supers. I'm sorry that I didn't tell you about it. I screwed up."

"Hank never did have sense about women. I wonder if he'll start trying to find Arlene," I said.

"Now you're worrying about Hank?" Jeremy asked me, almost but not quite incredulous.

"I don't think Hank's a bad guy deep down, and Arlene, who knows what her story is? It can't be good. She's not getting wealthy on vintage clothes, is she? And my guess is her acting career isn't going well either, if she is really an actress, which I seriously doubt, by the way."

"You don't have to do that," he said quietly.

"Worrying? Or getting a migraine? Or both?"

"Pretending that you're not angry when you are. I know you're angry that I haven't come back more often. I know I screwed up about the clothes."

"I'm not pretending. This is me, *angry*. This is how I am, this. I don't throw fits or scream or weep or whatever it is that you think women do. Anyway, it is not like there is a single thought running through my head. There are different thoughts. Anger is in there but it's not at the front. Maybe it's in the middle, squeezed between some others."

"What others?" he asked, and he looked unhappy.

"I'm thinking about my research and whether I'm going in the wrong direction with it. I'm thinking that you never ask about that, not once. I'm thinking that you have the money, but you never sent me an airline ticket. Even though you know I can't afford it. And I'm thinking that you told Francois Morel that it was luck about your working with Sky, like it had nothing to do with me. I don't know how to think about that—that you didn't thank me."

"But it was luck. I'm not some prodigy. I wouldn't have a clue how to get a director to look at my writing. That's what I meant: Having you was luck."

"Actually, that is why you thank people, Jeremy," I said, trying not to raise my voice. "Your way of thanking me was to move out to L.A. without talking to me and forgetting about my clothes, which is why Arlene tried them on. That is not how you thank people. You do not throw out their stuff and then act like it's funny. That is not a good thank you."

He looked at me, wide-eyed as a schoolboy. "I missed the chapter on politeness formulas." He waited until I cracked a smile, as he knew I always did.

"Well, it is an invaluable resource, as we know," I replied.

Then he kissed me again and again, on my eyelids, all over. Jeremy never cared who was around. "No, you are," he whispered. "I miss you. I miss this, all of this."

I whispered back, as if I was afraid that he might hear me. "I love you, but it shouldn't feel this hard. I don't know what to do, Jeremy," I told him.

"I think I do," he said, lifting my chin so that our eyes met.

"What do you think?" I asked.

"Maybe we should get married," he said.

Perhaps it was the onset of the migraine or all that strange talk about Hank and Arlene, but I had trouble getting it straight. I answered slowly, as if translating from a foreign tongue. "You're saying maybe we should get married, like, to one another."

"No, I mean let's marry different people and date each other on the side. It will be fun. We can go on double dates." He laughed, and said, "Of course, you and I, who else?"

"Well, it's a relief that you're not marrying Arlene. That's a good thing."

He kissed me again, this time on my lips. "I don't think that would work out."

"Probably not," I said. "And I never cared much for Hank, to be honest."

"No," he said.

"So that leaves you and me, I guess."

"Yes, Bella, that leaves us."

"I'd need to learn to drive," I told him. "Maybe, we could do it next year, maybe in the spring, once I know how to parallel park, things like that. I guess I need a driver's permit and then I have to take a test."

"You're good at tests," he said.

"Maybe," I replied.

# FIFTEEN

It's a strange thing about life. You keep chasing things, hoping to catch them, and then when you do, it feels different, not exactly a letdown, but different. I'd expected something like bliss if Jeremy asked me to marry him—with my biggest headaches being the size of our guest list and the content of our vows. I'd even memorized a few quotes from the Bard for the occasion. "Love is not love which alters when it alteration finds"—I should have given some thought to that one.

But there's that other saying—the best laid plans of mice and men oft go a-something?

Instead of bells ringing, my ears were ringing. My heart was racing. I had nightmares about buildings toppling and crushing me. If everything had been back to normal—that is, no marriage proposal—Jeremy could have calmed me. But naturally, that was out. It's not as if you call your boyfriend and whisper, "Oh, I'm so happy that I'm having panic attacks!" It takes the bloom off the rose, so to speak.

But marriage or no, I needed a driver's license. Academic life was one big lottery: I could land anywhere. Perhaps I'd be one of the chosen few who could work in New York or another walkable city, but that was not a given. Most teaching jobs, especially the good ones, were in college towns like Princeton or Bloomington— pleasant, even idyllic, but not without a car. If I were going to stay in the game, I'd have to learn to drive.

As Jeremy had known, there were driving schools for laggards like me who had reached the ancient age of twenty-six without a driver's license. One ad immediately caught my eye: "Special Attention to Nervous Drivers."

"We help people like you every day," an understanding voice said, as if soothing a hysterical mental patient.

My instructor was a skinny young guy named Dwayne who dressed in a brown suit and bright flowered tie, with a name tag, too. He opened the door for me with a grandiose flourish and said, "Dwayne is going to get you that driver's license, no problem. That is what Dwayne does. That is what he is here for. So, tell me, why aren't you driving? You had some sort of accident, like your bones were broken and your face was smashed?"

"No," I assured him. "No accident."

"Understood. You got some kind of phobia, like Dwayne's cousin, he's all scared of spiders," said Dwayne with unabashed enthusiasm.

"It's more than that. It's kind of the entire physical world, like the whole material experience, you know. Like I'm not good at running or hanging curtains, I'm more…spiritual, you could say, except not in a going-to-church way. But yes, I guess I do think cars are super-lethal death traps, now that you mention it."

Dwayne nodded. "That's good news," he declared.

"It doesn't seem like good news, survival-wise. Actually, it sounds like bad news."

"It's dangerous out there," he announced gleefully. "Good to know that at the start, because if you do not, you get into trouble, like with your car on the side of the highway."

"Oh," I said.

"But don't worry. Once you get the hang of defensive driving, you are one step ahead of the competition. That is what Dwayne is going to teach you, see where I'm going? It's good to see cars as killers because they are, especially where I'm from in North Philly. There, it's all one big mind game. Every time you're out there, you got to think, someone's out to kill me. But trust Dwayne, he will protect you. By the way, today you're getting your driver's permit, and getting started, all in one morning. It's our economy special."

He handed me a book, which was in fact a *Pennsylvania Driver's Manual*. It was filled with odd hieroglyphics that were, apparently, the lingua franca of the road. Arrows pointing one way, then another, squares and triangles, all intended to be clearer than English instructions like uphill or downhill—but which signaled nothing to the untutored eye.

"Study as we go," Dwayne said cheerfully. "Like, what do you do if you're driving through an intersection? Do you go as fast as you can?"

"I don't think that would be the right answer," I replied.

"That's right. Take your time, enjoy the scenery. You see where Dwayne is going? Anytime a question has a choice, you pick 'slow and look out for those killer cars.' Trust Dwayne. You do that, and you pass."

By morning's end, I had the permit that had eluded me in my teen years. I scraped by, which is all the wise Commonwealth of Pennsylvania required of its future drivers. And we were off for my first official lesson in the art of turning the engine on and off.

I took to it, so I thought, like a duck to water.

"Turning on a car is really simple," I said as I let the engine roar. "You just put the key in, and it starts."

Dwayne offered a pained sort of smile. He took the keys from my hand, gently. "You are doing fine, but you see, you don't have to linger. Dwayne says: Turn it until you hear that sound. What you're doing there, that's called flooding the engine."

He showed me the correct procedure a few times, which I was miraculously able to copy. "Dwayne is an excellent teacher," I said, falling easily into his third person locution. "In one day, I got a permit and I know how to start an engine. I bet I could start any car, even a Jaguar or one of those cute little Porsches." I smiled as I pictured myself turning fancy red sports cars on and off, far from the madding freeway.

He looked at me fearfully. "Are you planning to drive for real, or just get your license? Dwayne doesn't like to pry. But it's the policy to understand the customer."

"Well, I might end up driving in a real car in a real city with cars. My boyfriend lives in L.A. and out there, no one walks."

"Dwayne's going to be straight with you. This here, this is all about getting your Pennsylvania driver's license. It's not about driving on expressways. That's a whole different package, whole different pricing structure."

"Bella understands," I said.

I had asked Dwayne to deposit me near school, but not too close to my department. I was hoping to avoid the inevitable driving-related inquiries—like why I never drove, or why I had to drive now. He opened the car door for me, with another one of his flourishes, at the moment that Jessica and Natasha were strolling down Walnut with Natasha's gargantuan barking Great Dane.

As he drove off, I faced the two of them. "Hello there," said Jessica. "Are you cheating on Jeremy with that adorable guy?"

"It so happens that I am taking official driving lessons," I said stiffly, "which is why we were in a car marked Student Driver."

"I guess you're investigating how driving instructors speak to students?" asked Jessica with apparent sincerity.

"My instructor does have an idiosyncratic approach to speech, now that you mention it," I said, Professor Higgins-style. "He speaks of himself in the third person."

"Interesting," observed Natasha. "There are probably a host of unique speech patterns in that context. You could compare female versus male instructors, could be interesting, not to mention social class-related differences. Maybe we could generate a grant." Since Natasha had gained fame for her landmark study, *Language Patterns and Dialects of Taxi Drivers*, she was all-aglow at the prospect.

Jessica, on autopilot, exclaimed, "We could learn a lot!" She leaned forward in unconscious imitation of Natasha.

"In my case, about learning how to drive," I said, haughtily. "I doubt that anyone wants to fund that, even the Federal government."

Natasha gave her well-coiffed head a few rapid shakes to clarify the situation. "Driving?" she asked. "You're taking lessons?"

"Yes, people take lessons to learn how to drive. That is why there are driving schools," I informed the incredulous duo. "They're actually not designed for ethno-linguistics research."

"Why don't you know how to drive?" asked Jessica.

"Probably a learning disability," I said. "Or maybe a deep phobia, which is what my instructor thinks."

"If you have such a phobia, why drive?" was her next, perfectly logical, query.

"First of all, it's not practical to lead a walking-only life in America, and second, I am terrified of bicycling in city traffic. And third, Jeremy asked me to marry him so I might move to L.A."

"Oh Bella!" said Jessica. She gave me a big celebratory smooch.

"Thanks, but I have a lot to figure out, a lot of variables, like driving and figuring out how to finish my dissertation research."

I stopped before I accidentally mentioned Francois Morel, who had no right being a variable, even an extraneous one.

# SIXTEEN

My driving test felt like a cozy family get-together: Many, if not most, of the hard-working men and women at Pennsylvania's Department of Motor Vehicles were cousins, friends of cousins, or otherwise related to Dwayne. I whizzed through three-point turns, parallel parking, and the odd task of weaving the car around cones lined up in the row. After a few grins and slaps on the back, I left, a driver at last—it had only taken a month.

I danced up the stairs to my brownstone, feeling all was right with the world—it was a bright sunny day, blue skies and puffy clouds. Birds somewhere were tweeting, if not in my immediate vicinity. In front of the door was a package addressed to me, from Saks in Los Angeles. I reasoned that Jeremy had done a little gift shopping. Although Saks didn't, as far as I knew, sell rings, it might offer classy lingerie.

This was a different order of gift, a silk dress that I recognized from the latest issue of *Vogue*—the kind that costs more than a spacesuit, and, in my view, way more than any earthly garment ought to cost. I was muttering "ridiculous" even before I saw the note: "It's not vintage, but I hope you like it. Love, Jeremy."

My frugality did not stop me from trying it on. I squeezed myself into sheer pantyhose, my highest heels, and slipped it on— a straight beige sheath that seemed flamboyantly stark and 180 degrees from my vintage prizes, with their rhinestone flourishes, red cherries, and tiny birds. My reflection suggested a girl wearing her mother's dress—not my mother, but some other mother who enjoyed beige. The best that could be said was that I resembled a First Lady, a job that, fortunately, would seem to have little place in my future. I took it off and hung it as carefully as a work of art, since it cost as much.

Jeremy called a little later to find out about my driving test, which I described in gruesome detail. There's only so much suspense that you can breathe into parallel parking. But he listened like a good sport, inserting the usual "that's great" along the way. At last, he said, "I hope you got the dress. I know it doesn't make up for the others, but I tried."

The pilfered vintage dresses were a touchy subject, but I tried my best to be sugary-sweet. "It's wonderful, but it's too expensive. You shouldn't have spent so much."

"Sky said that's what good dresses cost," he answered.

"Huh? He knows about designer dresses now?"

"Tatiana wears this label," Jeremy said. "The two of you are about the same size, and she always looks good."

I pictured the infinitely chic Tatiana Biro offering Euro-style fashion advice and looking "good." No version of that picture was acceptable, but for reasons that I could not share with Jeremy. "You went shopping with her?"

"No, she's in Paris trying to get that Bulgarian poet script of hers off the ground. Sky says she's found some European willing to fund it, if you can believe it."

"Well, there is the whole nation of Bulgaria. There's got to be one rich person there," I said.

"Probably not," said Jeremy.

"I can wear the dress to Sue's wedding. It is daytime, so it's dressy enough, and maybe we'll spend the weekend in New York." As I spoke, I was adding up a few hotel nights, plus plane ticket. I figured that the total came to about as much as the Saks dress.

"Do we have to?" Jeremy replied, yawning. "I can't stand Sue." In his case, I could have inserted almost any name, and his statement would be, sadly, true.

I tried to keep any edge out of my voice. "You promised that you'd fly back next month. I said yes for the two of us."

After a long pause, he said, as if inspired, "Say we both got the flu."

"Jeremy," I sighed.

"Bella," he replied, imitating me with an even louder sigh.

"You make everything so difficult."

"I do," he said, rather amiably. "And I love you."

Well, there was nothing to say after that, except "I love you, too." And with that, we ended the call.

I dreaded telling Sue. Her wedding had become a multinational event, with delays and accommodations for the Irish contingent. Sue's ever-thrifty mother had estimated the "cost-per-guest" down to the last bottle of Guinness, in order to fit in all of the Irish aunts, uncles, and cousins. Jeremy's no-show, to put it mildly, would be noted by the current Mrs. Olinsky, if not the future Mrs. Olinsky-Grace.

Better to put that conversation off, I thought.

In an act of what I can only term girlish compensation, I walked downtown to explore a new organic makeup salon on South Street. The store had been open a few weeks, but it was already jammed. I applied a maroon lipstick, worthy of Marlene Dietrich in her Blue Angel phase, and to top it off, a peach blush with a glittery element.

Call it a small world, but who should appear but none other than Drew Hayworth, whom I had last seen as one of the actress/waitresses at Aaron's Garden on Manhattan's Upper West Side? She wore a flimsy dress, a Yankees cap, and ornately decorated cowboy boots that stopped at her ankles. A sight for sore eyes, I believe, is the expression.

She sidled over to me and said, "Hey there! That blush is great, you should buy it. And hello and how are you, of course."

"Drew," I said, nonplussed. "What are you doing here? I mean, are you living in Philly?"

"I'm doing a play at the Arden," she said. "It's a musical, and guess who has the female lead?"

"Wow, that's fantastic!"

"It's all about making the right choices," she said, turning misty-eyed. "I could have stayed in Manhattan and still be a waitress, which isn't why I went to NYU in the first place. I had to take control of my own destiny. It is such a Virgo thing. So here I am, in Philly, which is where I need to be for myself."

So Drew had progressed from controlling her hair to managing greater things, apparently with the assistance of the Zodiac.

"Great," I said.

"You and Jeremy should come see us," she said, "That is, if you guys are still together." She handed me a brightly colored flyer, which I slid into my pocket.

"I'm here in grad school, and he's in L.A., working on a film, but yeah, we're together," I said.

"You fly back and forth?" she asked, applying some glitter to her lids, which made her eyes look even starrier.

"Not a lot," I said. I might have said, never, but I figured that "not a lot" summed it up nicely.

"Hmm," she said.

I guess, what with all the chatter about Sue's wedding, that I had weddings on my brain. "But Jeremy did propose, so eventually we won't have to fly back and forth, which gets very tiring. We'll probably live together when we're married," I said and added rather loudly, "and we'll have a wedding."

"Be careful with your vows," she said. "Some of them make you want to shoot yourself. Last wedding I sang at, some older couple, and I do mean older, read from *Winnie the Pooh*. She said,

'How do you spell love?' And he said, 'You don't spell it, you feel it.'" Drew paused for theatrical effect. "They called each other Piglet and Pooh."

I pictured the two love-struck seniors, joyfully planning their Piglet and Pooh vows. Maybe they decorated their cake with sugary-pink piglets and tiny chocolate bears, and why not? Their kids probably felt like hiding under the table—but the couple had their Pooh day.

"I'd pick the quote about what I like doing best is nothing," I said. "But it isn't very romantic. Probably a vow should be like, 'What I like best is helping you be a better man.'"

"Not that Jeremy needs help in that department," said Drew.

"His dream vows are like vows of silence," I said, which was true enough. Beckett was more Jeremy's style, as opposed to *Winnie the Pooh*.

"So when's the big date?" she asked.

"Date?"

"The wedding date," she said, a little testily, I thought.

"Whose wedding?"

"You're getting married," she reminded me. "To Jeremy."

"Right, but it's kind of a secret right now," I said.

Then we exchanged phone numbers and a cool set of pecks.

# SEVENTEEN

Francois kept his door locked except during office hours. But I'd gotten into the habit of visiting him at the end of the day when no one was around. I tapped softly; he'd know who it was.

He opened his door and said, "Ah, I've just been reviewing your paper."

"I hope you're not disappointed," I said, but I knew that he wasn't.

"In you, never," he said, looking at me with his serious eyes. "You let the data guide you. Most people are too eager to be right. They cling to pet theories."

"It's hard to be wrong. You put a lot of time and effort into one theory, one direction. You're sure you're right. But I was on the wrong path, for sure."

"This is what your dissertation should focus on, this idea that kids acquire empathy from narratives, not words. It's original."

I said, "It's my dissertation that I wanted to talk to you about."

"No rush. I am putting together a conference session in Boston and I'd like you to prepare a paper. I like Boston, it's a civilized city. Next spring, it's very nice, a little cool still."

"Next year, you mean?" I asked nervously.

"Is there a conflict?"

"I might be moving to L.A. Jeremy asked me to marry him. I passed my driver's test." I tried to smile, but somehow my lips were not moving in the right direction.

"You're not asking Jeremy to give up Hollywood, are you?" he asked.

"It's not the same. I'm the reason that Jeremy's in L.A. I chased Sky Lowe down and forced him to read Jeremy's stories. I wouldn't take 'no' for an answer, and then Sky wanted Jeremy to be in L.A., which I never expected. So this is my fault."

"Ah," he said. "Bella, switching graduate programs isn't that simple. It's not like transferring as an undergraduate. Once we're at this level, there are few programs that can fund you, if any. It's as limited as Hollywood, just not as lucrative. Things happen at certain times, in certain schools. Besides, married couples commute. It's common."

"But it's not what Jeremy wants. He wants me with him in L.A.," I said, unhappily.

"But I want you here," he said. "I'm asking you to stay here."

As it had before, his directness took me by surprise. He asked for what he wanted and nothing else. There was no hidden agenda. Still, I told him, "I don't think you have that right."

"I didn't say I had a right, I said I was asking," he replied.

"That's not fair, I'm confused enough," I said. "Don't make this harder for me."

"It's not a command. You'll do what you like. Both of us know that. And whatever you decide, I will help you. There's no quid pro quo, please understand. If you decide to move to L.A., I will do everything in my power to help—references, phone calls, any favor I can offer, whatever you want. But…" he stopped and gave a helpless, almost apologetic, shrug.

"But what?"

"It would break my heart," he said.

I heard voices down the hall from another office. There was laughter and then footsteps down the stairs. I had stopped breathing, and it seemed Francois had as well. I waited until the sounds subsided and the hallway was noiseless again. I almost opened the door, but I hated to, more than anything in the world.

"I should go now," I said, but I didn't.

"Today is my birthday. You could have dinner with me and we could talk more. Anyway, I'm all alone tonight."

Maybe it was the way he said "alone" that made me hesitate. "I don't know how old you are or where you were born," I said.

"I am thirty-six and I was born in Brest. That's a not very large town on the coast of the Atlantic in the North of France. Most people don't know it, but it's beautiful."

"And I'm twenty-six and I was born in New York," I told him. "And yes, I'll have dinner with you, Francois."


We met at a small restaurant not too far from where I lived. Back then, Philadelphia had lots of young ambitious chefs from The Restaurant School—and there was an out-of-the-way place called Jason's, beneath the Market Street Bridge. On a whim, or maybe more, I decided to wear my new silk dress.

I looked around. I saw a foreign-looking man with longish dark hair, a bony face, pale skin. It took more than a few seconds for me to recognize him. Even though I had arrived early, I knew that he had been waiting. As I crossed the room, he rose, and pulled out a chair.

He said, "You look beautiful."

A few hours earlier, I'd felt something like dowdy. But whether it was the new lipstick or the candlelit room or the compliment, I felt anything but.

I let him do the ordering. When our waiter came over, Francois rattled off a few dishes, ordered a bottle of wine, and then turned his attention to me. He barely touched my fingertips and said, "Thank you for coming tonight."

I said, "I wouldn't want to think of you having dinner alone."

He said, lightly, "I usually do. But I don't mind."

"You must mind a little," I said. "People don't get married to have dinner alone."

"I can't speak for most marriages. I've been busy—getting tenure, publishing, research. I didn't think my marriage was any worse than most. Maybe it wouldn't be, if Tatiana were less…public."

"Things like that burn out. You said so yourself," I said. "She'll get bored with Sky Lowe eventually. I like Sky, but he's not you."

"I'm boring enough," he laughed. "Anyway, tonight has nothing to do with anything but you. I never expected…something that's not like lightning, but like light."

I let his words run over me, like waves.

And after a while, he said, "I'm glad you're here. I hope you are, too."

"I wouldn't want to be anywhere else. And this food is kind of amazing, whatever it is. It's delicious."

"It's a bouillabaisse. My mother makes a nice version. Here, they use anise, it gives it a little kick," he said. "Does your mother make you special dishes?"

I felt it best not to describe my mother's absence of culinary talents—which brought to mind Levi Strauss's opus, *The Raw and the Cooked*. "I wouldn't call them special," I said. "Our family was more into Chinese takeout. It's an old Jewish tradition, egg rolls and wonton soup."

All of my preconceptions about him turned out to be wrong. He wasn't from a sophisticated city like Paris, as I'd imagined, but from Brittany. As a boy, he had dreamed of becoming a naval engineer, like his father. He came from a large family of aunts and uncles and scores of cousins. Doting parents. He choked up speaking about his father's sacrifices. He adored his musician mother, his brilliant younger sisters. It was like *Life with Father* in Brittany.

"You must have some neuroses," I said. "Your family sounds too perfect. Weren't there hidden cracks under the surface?"

He seemed puzzled. "Not at all. My parents are educated, kind. I had nothing to be neurotic about. I don't understand this American idea of blaming fathers and mothers. It's unpleasant and perverse, I think."

"Freud was a German and he wrote the book on parents, so it's not an American concept, and no one's blaming anyone," I said. Now was not the ideal moment to let Francois know that I called my mother every day.

"Freudian theory is nonsense. He wasn't a real scientist and his views of women were absurd," said Francois dismissively. "You're not neurotic. Wasn't your childhood normal?"

"No one was hanging themselves in the attic, if that's what you mean," I said. "I guess I was kind of in my own orbit."

"Lots of children are shy," he said.

"No, it was more than that," I said. "Maybe there's a switch— it either gets turned on or it doesn't. And it never got turned on, so that people made sense to me, not just their words, but what's really behind the words. And I never made sense to them. Maybe I'm still waiting. That probably doesn't make sense."

"You make perfect sense to me," he said, taking my hand.

Afterward, the night was warm, and the streets deserted, and we lingered outside my door, our faces lit up by the street lamps and neither of us wanting to move. I asked him, "Are you going to kiss me goodnight?"

And he whispered, "Am I?"

# EIGHTEEN

By some standards, nothing much had happened—one kiss, a soft kiss that felt as natural as breathing. But a year's history went into that kiss—and it hit me like a blast of unsuspected joy, like a rainbow. Afterward, everything had changed.

I wasn't the same, and it wasn't Jeremy's fault.

I gave myself a stern lecture: he's married, he's your professor, it can't go anywhere. But that's the problem with advice; it's easy to dole out, but hard to take.

Still, whatever happened, Jeremy wouldn't leave empty-handed. I'd won him a job, and it wasn't any old office job. He couldn't stay bitter after he had racked up a few Oscars, could he? Later, when he was older, wiser, and, of course, still incredibly good-looking, he might get nostalgic. He'd show a picture of me to his kids, all of whom would inherit his dark dreamy eyes and curly hair and would be brilliant besides, winning Nobel Prizes and going to Harvard. I preferred to leave the wife role blank—although obviously, he'd require help in order to produce genius offspring.

Anyway, our middle-aged years were a long way off. Now was the season of our discontent. No matter how I sliced it, it was a mess. My mess.

Meanwhile, I took a good hard look at my apartment—and when I say "good," I mean the way a man like Francois might view it. How had I lived this way? My two small closets were one mass of cloudlike dust-balls. Enough spiderwebs under the tables and chairs for an entire insect zoo. Whatever was in my refrigerator belonged in a food museum: two blackened bananas and some mystery substances wrapped in tinfoil. The bathroom was beyond civilized discussion, but not, mercifully, beyond the powers of a bottle of bleach.

Jeremy didn't care, or even notice, any more than he took notice of tables or chairs. Jeremy liked the mess, the messy parts of me, the parts that didn't fit anywhere but with him. If he had seen the black bananas, he might improvise a skit about them on the spot.

Francois was different. He was older, for one thing—not old by any stretch, but older than I was, with a taste for the good life. But more than that, Francois admired me. He didn't imagine me living with rotting fruit or dust, and it was up to me to prove him right. Somewhere underneath all of my shoeboxes was a Hoover, no doubt in pristine condition, given that I'd never used it. Surely it had one of those instruction manuals.

Hours later found me knee-deep in housework, and the buzzer rang. I ran downstairs to find a FedEx guy, holding a package in a self-important way. "Package from Sky Lowe Productions—it's marked 'Confidential,'" he informed me, loving every second of it. It's not every day that a Philly FedEx guy gets to deliver a Hollywood package.

Judging from the way his wide smile evaporated, my soiled T-shirt and baggy jeans were a big letdown. It's like Coco Chanel (or someone famous) said, you never know when you need to be dressed. The FedEx guy turned official and handed me a ballpoint to sign for the package.

"This is exciting, getting a FedEx. It's my second FedEx in my whole life," I confessed. "I'm confused why people don't use the regular mail. It doesn't take very long, does it? I guess a day sometimes really matters."

"That's why we're in business," he said grimly. Maybe he thought I was trying to rob him of his speedy livelihood.

"Many people need you, I'm sure," I said. But he looked glad to see the last of me, especially in my filthy clothes.

I was upstairs in a flash to open the package. Inside, I found what looked to be the working script for *Scared Jim*. Sky, or an overly diligent intern, had marked every single page with "Confidential" in big red letters. That seemed like Hollywood overkill, since no one whom I knew was dying to read it. Probably one of those legal things, I imagined, in case I stole the idea and made my own movie, like *Grad School Jim*.

Sky had handwritten a note on official stationery:

Dear Bella, Call me after you read it and I will explain. Don't worry about the time difference—I never do. Later, Sky

I confess to a tiny thrill. Well, actually, a giant surge. Yes, Jeremy had been writing with Sky for months. I had met Sky. Still, this was a genuine Hollywood script, sent to me of all people, a lowly grad student.

But I also had a queasy feeling. Jeremy shared his writing with me, which is how I'd read the stories in the first place. Yet, up to today, I hadn't seen a single page of the screenplay for *Scared Jim*. Not one. Plus, he had made a glib, offhand remark about his script not being "really" scary. That was a Stop Sign, a blinking red light for a horror movie. If a horror movie isn't frightening, then what is it?

All was not well on the Western Front.

Jeremy had filled me in on "the business" as he called it. Getting dumped was par for the course: Screenwriters came and went, replaceable cogs in a fast-moving machine. "It's a supply/demand issue. Hundreds of writers for every slot, not much difference between them in terms of talent—there's zero security," he said.

"But they're your stories," I insisted. "Sky wouldn't do that to you."

"Yeah, he would," Jeremy said.

I cleaned as I read. The vacuum's humming almost drowned out, but not quite, the noise in my head. I was trying not to worry about Jeremy's future. But the script was of little help in that regard.

—On page 1, a large tiger chased Jim in a jungle that turned into a prison. It wasn't a real chase, it was a dream.

—On page 5, there was a flashback to the Boer War, with very drunk soldiers who sang in Afrikaans. It wasn't a real flashback, it was a dream.

—On page 20, Jim was drowning in an octagonal swimming pool that turned out to be inside of a spaceship (page 40), which turned out to be a prison (page 60).

—On page 80, Jim made his first escape. Since I was still a free woman, I took the liberty of skipping ahead to where an old ugly woman died, or maybe she didn't.

I kept on turning the vacuum cleaner off and writing myself notes, as if for an academic paper. I scribbled my questions:

Maybe a dream within a dream?

Is this a flashback within a flashback?

Confusion: Is this yesterday or the future?

Confusion: Is the escape a dream or real or a flashback?

Old woman: Is she grandmother or witch?

My list might have formed the basis for one of those modernist plays, which seem to have no beginning or end, or, for that matter, middle. I had a momentary bleak vision of a lifetime spent analyzing *Scared Jim*. Luckily, I was not enrolled in a cinema studies department and I decided that my list was long enough for all practical purposes. I worked up the nerve to call Sky and hoped for the best.

"Bella," he said, sounding as if he had a bad cold. "So what did you think?"

"It's…challenging," I began. "It's sort of a departure from Jeremy's stories. I mean, his plots are tight. And this is looser, actually, a lot looser, sort of free flowing almost, almost like a stream of consciousness."

"I tried to get him to push the envelope, make it dark and edgy. At first, he fought me, but I like creative conflict."

"It is edgy," I agreed.

"Very edgy," he said. He sneezed a few times.

"And dark, it is dark."

"Very dark," he said. "But I'm wondering, is it too dark for kids? Maybe it's kind of seriously dark, like really dark, like way too dark."

I pictured hordes of teary-eyed kids running, terrified, from the movie theater, their mothers scrambling after them—or, more likely, row after row of peacefully napping youngsters and moms. Neither scenario boded well for future box office.

"Maybe it is a tad dark…for kids," I said.

"So, give me your gut reaction, top-of-mind. Excuse me, I'm getting some tea."

I collected my thoughts. It was critical to act natural, as if nothing were at stake. "Sky, I've never read a screenplay. This is the first time I've even seen the words 'Interior' and 'Exterior.' I could be way off base."

"I trust you. Be totally honest. Be brrrrutal."

As any halfwit knows, no sane person, under any circumstances, desires brutal honesty, unless that honesty consists of fawning, like, gee, how brilliant is that? Besides, the last thing that I wanted to be was "brutal" about my boyfriend's script, even if he might end up in the ex-boyfriend bin. Bad enough that I had looked into another man's eyes, I wasn't about to insult Jeremy's writing—I didn't blame him for the mess. But whatever the cause, *Scared Jim* was a disaster of epic proportions, which Sky knew, or he wouldn't have sent me the script—why me, I couldn't fathom.

I gave it my best shot. "Sky, this might be dark or edgy, but it's not scary. Most horror movies like *Village of the Damned*, they're linear. When there's a twist like in *Carnival of Souls*, it's foreshadowed. There has to be enough reality so weird stuff sticks out—like if everyone's crazy in a lunatic asylum, it's not scary. It's only scary if one person is sane, but he's stuck with all the crazies. If everything's fantasy, there's nothing to wake up to."

"You're pretty good at this, Bella. You could work in movies."

"But that's not my goal," I reminded him.

"Just saying, is all. Anyway, does this feel like a story? Does it hang together?"

"Well it's more experimental, off the beaten track, like one of those Godard films. New Wave Cinema."

"So you're thinking it's more for teens?"

"I wouldn't say all teens," I said, "no, not all."

"But most?" he asked, with a hopeful tone.

"I wouldn't go that far—maybe not most teens. Take the Boer War. That's maybe a little…you know, it's not a big war like the Civil War. Like you said about Bulgaria being a small country, the Boer War is a small war."

"It seemed like a very cool war."

"I think cool wars are like *Star Wars*, not wars where people died," I said. "If wizards are battling demons, that's a fun war. The Boer War, the Crimean War, those wars aren't cool. They're sort of obscure, tragic wars that no one learns about in school."

He paused to absorb this insight and then sneezed. "Got ya," he said.

"Anyway, what I think doesn't count. You are making this for boys—I never was a boy or even a tomboy or even slightly boyish. I was more into Jane Austen."

"Hey, I like Jane Austen."

"You do?" I asked, shocked.

"Man, I love Jane Austen. She's terrific."

Now, let's face it, most grown men do not admit to an affection for Jane—in fact, probably even fewer than the brainy military-minded teens who study the Boer War. I doubted that Jeremy could plow through fifty pages of *Emma* without extreme mental fatigue—and it was hard to picture Francois taking time away from his elaborate experiments to dip into *Pride and Prejudice*. Sky Lowe was his own man, to be sure. Even coughing and wheezing, I liked him. We got along.

"Sky, you should talk to real kids. You could test storyboards or other concepts with real people. You can test references like, well, the Boer War, if you're dead set on it."

"So, we're on the same page," Sky said, sniffing.

"We are?" I asked, confused.

"Definitely. You can help me. I have the storyboards, I have plenty of money, and I know the way the university works," he said. "That is, if you're willing."

I could detect the hand of Professor Natasha Lowenstein in molding this scenario. Outright nepotism aside, it wasn't the worst idea.

"I'm guessing your family connections played a role?"

"Natasha and I talked about this," he said.

"No kidding. Seriously, why me? Hundreds of people in L.A. could do this."

"Call it a hunch," he answered. "You had the instinct to get me the *Scared Jim* stories."

"That doesn't count. I only did it for Jeremy."

"And because you had a hunch, right?"

"I did," I said. "But Jeremy's going to hate this idea of testing."

"I don't want to hear that, it's not his film," Sky answered, switching to Hollywood in a flash. "He got points up front in this deal, by the way."

"Is it okay for me to say that I have no clue what you mean?"

"Percentage points, Bella, I gave him a cut before we take out the costs, which is a very good deal. Bottom line, if the film makes money, so does Jeremy. If it makes lots of money, your man gets rich," he said. "So, how about it?"

I didn't grasp his answer about "points" or "upfront" except in a foggy way, but I got the point about money. Sky was a weird mix—ruthless without being nasty, ambitious but still generous. Dark, edgy, pushing the envelope, those were about box office hype. If Sky thought that refined made more money, he would do *Mansfield Park* in a heartbeat.

"The timing isn't great. Actually, it's horrible. I don't know where Jeremy and I are except maybe we live happily ever after or maybe we don't. But it's not going to happen in the way that Jeremy wants. I'm not ready to leave Philadelphia," I told him.

"So your relationship is kind of unconventional," he said.

"Maybe," I admitted, "a little."

"Guess it's kind of off the beaten track, sort of like one of those French New Wave movies, like *Jules and Jim.* Is that what you're saying?"

"It's what you're saying." I laughed. "Promise me that you won't say anything to Jeremy about this."

"I'm cool," said Sky after a few coughs. "So you'll do this? I can figure out the grant part with the school. There's a lot of paperwork but Natasha can handle that."

"You pay the school and I get the exact same stipend that I'm already getting, not a penny extra."

"The Rules of the Game," he said—to which he did not, mercifully, add "cool title."

"So I do have one condition, Sky. It's 100% non-negotiable in your lingo."

"Shoot," he said.

"We know there's going to be a rewrite," I began.

"I haven't said that," Sky interrupted.

"No, there's going to be a rewrite and we both know it, a major rewrite."

"OK, so what's your condition? You want a credit, I guess. Not a problem. You deserve it."

"Sky, a movie credit doesn't help an academic career unless it's a documentary for PBS, and we know I can't accept money," I said. "What I want—it's all that I want—is for Jeremy to write the next draft. You can bring in another writer later, but not now. Plus, he gets writer's credit."

"What I Did for Love," Sky sang, mangling the tune from *A Chorus Line*. "Is that about it?" he asked.

"Yup," I said. "Give me your word, Sky."

"I'm a romantic. You have my word."

Funny, but with all this cleaning and fretting, I hadn't glanced at the flyer that gorgeous Drew handed me. Now my eyes happened to fall upon it—neon bright, with kooky bold lettering.

"Another thing, Sky, and this has nothing to do with me," I said. "Maybe it's something and maybe it's nothing. I was buying makeup today and I met this woman from New York, which is kind of funny in a way."

"Small world," he said, coughing.

"Exactly, it is a small world. The point is, this woman, Drew Hayworth, is performing in a play downtown. She's an actress."

"Which is why she's in a play," added Sky to help me along.

"Exactly, she's an actress and so she's in a play and she passed me the flyer for the play, which seems to be a gay musical."

"Nothing wrong with that," he croaked.

"Nothing wrong, of course not. And obviously, the flyer has the name of the musical on it. That's what you expect on a flyer, the title."

"All about the title," he declared. "Like *Scared Jim*, that's a cool title. We got toys and coffee cups, all kinds of stuff with that name on it—everything's *Scared Jim*."

"Exactly, that's the point, Sky. The title of this gay musical is *Scared Jim*."

# NINETEEN

I was humming a bit of "It Might as Well Be Spring" when the evening began. I did have more than a bit of spring fever, and it wasn't even spring—it was early summer with a vengeance in Philadelphia. Apart from dreaming about Francois, I had a soft spot for musicals of the 1950s perky variety, and this one seemed to fit the bill. There was a good-sized crowd for the preview of *Scared Jim: The Musical*—mostly men wearing tight sexy T-shirts, red bandanas in back pockets.

Sky Lowe, though, was in a funk—he faced the wall, hiding. After *Kill More or Die!*, Sky was a minor celebrity, so he had a right to be cautious. But he looked downright awful and, if possible, more slovenly than usual—short a month's sleep, a shave, and perhaps a personal trainer.

I asked, "Are you alright? Or are you still angry about the title?"

"No, it's Tatiana," he sighed. "She said no again."

Sky Lowe's marriage proposals were a fixed element in his ongoing Tatiana saga. Sky was hell-bent on becoming Husband Number Three, although why was beyond me, considering how Tatiana insulted Husband Number One and cheated on Husband Number Two.

"You're skipping a few steps," I said. "Tatiana is already married."

"So is her husband," said Sky. "Francois Morel is married too."

He gave me one of those eagle-eyed looks—and I admit that part of me, a big part, wanted to tell all. Sky was brotherly, and given his pursuit of Tatiana, he couldn't judge me for one kiss. But confiding in Sky led straight to Jeremy and Natasha Lowenstein, and they were off limits. Everyone whom I knew was off limits, come to think of it.

"Europeans have a different approach to marriage," I said, trying to steer the discussion onto safer, if not entirely secure, ground.

"Europeans," he replied, eyeing me suspiciously.

"It's like this. American girls dream about finding the right man, someone who is super-handsome and super-smart, and marrying him. But in Europe, girls get married first, and then they dream about finding the right guy, kind of in reverse. It's a cultural difference, I think."

"Right," he said.

"Probably a holdover from the time marriages were arranged," I theorized, "and women were merely a form of property."

"Right," said Sky. "Listen. Tatiana's been talking."

"There's not much to tell," I said.

He looked at me, warily, and said, "Bella, 'not much' isn't nothing."

I could have kicked myself. But I'd never lied about anything, much less my heart. I was used to blathering to everyone like love-struck Freddie Eynsford-Hill in *My Fair Lady*, shouting about the towering feeling on the street where she lived. I could have played Freddie with conviction.

We made our way to the front row, where we had three seats—one was for Jeremy. But the seat stayed empty, like a reproach.

The play turned out to be a bouncy comedy of the sort that I usually relished. It was a true boy-meets-saucy-debutante-and-then-meets-her-even-saucier-brother sort of romp, with rousing songs, clever rhymes, and a happy ending. Drew, in the role of the wisecracking almost-girlfriend, was not half-bad—her voice was sultry, her legs a mile long, plus she had old-fashioned stage presence.

I imagine, from the way that the audience laughed from start to finish, that the production was more or less a joke-fest. But I wasn't laughing. I kept looking at Jeremy's seat. I wondered what he knew, when he knew, how much he knew—while cursing myself, over and over. I replayed the hypotheticals. If only x had not happened, then y would not have. But there were far too many x-events—if I hadn't met Francois, if I hadn't accepted the *Figaro* tickets, if I hadn't pressured Sky into hiring Jeremy, if, if, if…and there were those "interaction effects"—unintended effects that spoiled everyone's forecast, like Tatiana knowing Jeremy, Sky knowing Francois, in fact everyone knowing everyone. It was a tangled web, for sure.

The audience went wild at the conclusion and the standing ovation lasted forever, despite the heat. I said to Sky, "I wonder what happened to Jeremy."

"He's been moody," said Sky, and catching my frustrated expression, added, "I meant, moodier."

We'd planned one of those after-theater dinners at a nearby bar that seemed acceptably casual. The idea was that Drew and her producer would pop in and join us. That way, there was the pretense that the meeting was social, rather than the prelude to a straight cash-for-title deal. I guess that made everyone feel okay about the money part.

Sky was on L.A. time, so it was normal dinnertime for him. He ordered a bottle of Mexican beer. "We might as well wait," he said. "Try Negro Modelo, you'll like it."

I'd been too edgy all day to eat. Now, it hit me that I needed food or I would faint, not instantly, but soon. I asked the waitress, "Is it possible to get some bread, like a basket?"

The waitress regarded me quizzically and said, "You want a basket."

I tried again, "A basket with bread."

"Oh, bread," she said loftily. She seemed to treat my request as a future goal to be achieved in the fullness of time, as it were.

"I know lots of people aren't doing carbohydrates, but I'm okay with them," I said. "If you don't have bread, rolls are fine. Even breadsticks would work."

She wandered off with a lifeless gait, as if discouraged by my request. I briefly contemplated following her into the kitchen in order to plead for my rights as a customer.

But Drew Hayworth swept into the bar, stole two bowls of peanuts, grabbed a draft beer, winked at the sexy bartender, and sat down next to Sky. Before you could say boo, she was pouring Sky's beer and expounding upon her technique, which had something to do with tilting the glass or tilting the bottle, one or the other. Sky, like Jeremy, was a diehard Yankees fan and about the last man who could resist a stunning redhead in a Yankees cap.

They were soon arguing about games, series, balls, strikes, and pitches, and a man of an unpleasant, even evil, nature who, I surmised, was the team's manager.

"I could kill him," said Drew bitterly.

"Yeah, it's painful," Sky answered.

Their fierceness came as a shock. I'd thought of baseball as a carefree and wholesome sport. But the dark beer wasn't bad, and my mind soon floated to other, more pleasing, thoughts, like the way Francois Morel's long-fingered hands felt on the back of my neck, and how I had turned my face upwards to his. And, at that moment, or so it seemed, fingertips did brush against my shoulders.

"Oh," I said and swiveled around, wondering how on Earth Francois had found me, and if he'd ever tasted this delicious Mexican beer.

But it was not Francois. It was Jeremy, which I should have known. He had a good reason to be here, and Francois didn't have any.

"It's you," I said, trying to mask my confusion, or perhaps my disappointment. I couldn't figure out which.

"It is," he replied stiffly.

He sat down and eyed me like a suspect in a lineup. I gave him a kiss that did not seem to do the trick.

"Hey, how did you find us?" asked Sky. "We weren't sure if you were coming."

Jeremy said, "It was the closest place to the Arden." He signaled the waitress and ordered himself a Heineken like it was no big deal. I'd never seen Jeremy order an alcoholic beverage, much less a beer with a brand name.

Drew said, "Jeremy drinking, who'd have thought? And hello, it's been a while."

Jeremy smiled at her, which was his version of hello and how have you been. "It's hot in L.A.," he said, holding up the beer bottle.

Drew held up her beer bottle, too. "Cheers," she said.

Sky said, "Drew was fantastic. The audience just ate her up."

"It's a shame Jeremy missed you," I added to Drew—at the time, I imagined that she was a friend.

"Oh, that is a shame," she said in a demure manner—and, maybe it was my imagination, but it seemed as if she fluttered her eyelashes. "Jeremy, you're a real writer now, aren't you?"

"I get paid to write," he said, "so I guess that makes me a real writer."

She leaned toward him. "Tell me, what's a funny word for scared? I mean, our title is *Scared Jim*, and you know why we're all here, and you are a writer."

Jeremy began inspecting the menu. "You mean, what's a funny title. Let's see. *Timid Jim,* that's funny, it's got an internal rhyme, it's a little feminine. That would work. Or *Jittery Jim, Jim's Jitters, Jim Jinxes.* I'd probably go with *Timid Jim.*" He put down his menu. "Are we ready to order?"

Sky Lowe blinked more than once, and, imitating his academic sibling, shook his head a few times. He repeated, "*Timid Jim, Timid Jim....*That's a cool title, very cool."

"Totally," said Drew. "You are amazing, Jeremy."

I asked, "Why didn't you tell anyone that you had another title?"

Jeremy gave me a sharp look and said, "No one's tested it yet." And he flagged the waitress who, seeing a handsome man, perked up.

Orders were taken for hamburgers of various degrees of doneness—Jeremy's well done, mine medium.

"No bun for me," Drew announced. "Bread really slows me down."

The waitress gave me an angry look, as if to say, "Ha! And you had the audacity to ask for more bread!" I suppose that explains her failure to deliver even a cracker. Sky let her know that a burger was fine for him, too, with the lethargy-causing bun and all—and she waddled off to bother other customers.

"You know, Sky, I used to be a waitress. That's how I met these two. I had such a terrible crush on Jeremy," Drew said, and then turning to Jeremy, "I can confess, right? Now that you're going to be a married man?"

I may not know much about women, but this much I have learned: Women do not confess to crushes that are long dead unless the man's dead, too (movie stars being an exception, since crushes on George Clooney do not count). But if the fellow is alive, which Jeremy most certainly was, and the woman's talking, chances are it's an invitation, like "Oh, how I fancied you," to which he replies,

"Darling, if only I'd known." But true to form, Jeremy said nothing—and offered Drew one of his elusive smiles of the sort that produced her crush in the first place.

Sky slapped Jeremy on the back, and said, "Hey! I didn't know that you and Bella, well—that is just great! So, you guys have been keeping this a secret."

"It's not a secret," Jeremy said. "Obviously."

"Well, almost," I said. "I told a few people, not many. I mean, not my parents or anyone related to me, but I might have mentioned it."

"We could sync the wedding with the premiere," said Sky. "Maybe hire Drew to sing at your wedding."

"Ooh, I'd love that," Drew said, and snapped up a few more peanuts.

"I don't know that we've decided on the…wedding specifics," I said, and seeing Jeremy's hostile stare, I went on, "I mean, we could get married on a beach or on top of a mountain or on a cruise. I think couples in Japan travel to Disneyland with all their relatives, and they dress up as Snow White."

"Cool," said Sky, and Jeremy looked as if he'd lose it then and there.

Jeremy said, "Yes, Bella should dress up as Snow White."

Before the conversation got any tenser, *Scared Jim's* producer sauntered over to our table. He was a tall string-bean guy who acted as if he'd fallen off the plane from Kansas or some other place that has lots of cornfields, which, in his case, turned out to be Englewood, New Jersey.

"Hey, Drew, hey guys, Todd Seltzer," he said. "So, we got two productions and just one name. That is just plain crazy, just too crazy, ha ha." He recognized Sky and figured out who Jeremy was, so he turned to the last man (in a sense) standing, which was me. He said, "So, are you some kind of Hollywood producer, too?"

"I'm no one," I said. "I'm not important. I'm just here with…them."

Todd gave one of those man-of-the people, cornpone chuckles that he must have developed during his long and interesting years studying theater in New York. "Sure, you're here, nothing wrong with that. It's fine with me, just asking is all."

Sky said, "Bella's the one who gave me Jeremy's stories. She's the one who told me about your play…so, she's someone."

"Two pretty ladies, can't complain," said Todd, continuing the cornball act. "Guess it's my lucky night."

By the time our meals arrived, my appetite had fled. My burger tasted like bread with something in between, and the fries were hot for about thirty seconds, then limp. But the dark Mexican beer tasted fine, especially after the second.

There was an endless back-and-forth about scared versus timid, everyone fake jolly and fake rowdy. I was winding down in a serious way. Most nights, I was happily in dreamland by eleven. It was a stretch to keep my eyes open past midnight, even when Jeremy tried his best. No way was I going to last another hour— and I needed to be alone with Jeremy to find out what he knew or thought he knew.

I'd had enough. "Todd, listen. Jeremy's come up with a better title for your play. My guess is, whatever Sky offers, it's a good deal. You get a funnier title, plus you get cash, which, from where I'm sitting, makes sense. Sky, why don't you write down a number on your napkin, and Todd, if you're okay with it, we can order an after-dinner drink and all go home?"

Everyone choked as if I had made an off-color joke. Probably, if I'd shouted profanities at the top of my lungs, they wouldn't have been as shocked. I learned later to pretend that all films—even the ones that consist of high-rises exploding and men racing around, shrieking, "Hey Dude!"—are labors of love, and money a trivial, if necessary, side effect.

"I'm sorry if I wasn't supposed to mention money," I said. "But that's why we're all here, right? That's what they do in the movies, write things on napkins? Or are you supposed to go into a backroom and be top-secret about it? I don't think there's a backroom here."

Sky cracked up. "Bella, you are something."

"You're not only pretty, but real smart," said Todd, hee-hawing.

I grinned, matching his cornpone style, as if to say, gee, thanks, you're swell. Sure enough, Sky scribbled a number on his napkin, and passed it to Drew—who, without comment, handed it to Todd. In fact, it was just like one of those scenes in the movies. And after a brief glance, a gulp, and some rapid breathing, Todd nodded "yes" as if he might faint.

"It's a deal," said Sky, shaking Todd's hand heartily. Sky had no doubt sized him up from the first awful chuckle and paid him a paltry sum in Hollywood terms, but whatever the number, it was a fortune to a tiny play in Philly.

"Here's to *Timid Jim*," said Todd, ecstatically.

"Here's to *Scared Jim*," said Sky.

"Here's to Jeremy!" shouted Drew, and everyone clicked glasses.

Not to be outdone, Todd boomed, "Here's to Sky!" and we clicked again. Sky added a toast to me as well, for which I thanked him, although I was fast falling asleep.

The restaurant finally asked us, politely but firmly, to leave—Philadelphia not being such a late-night town in those days. I was saying my goodbyes when, from the corner of my eye, I caught Drew sidling over to Jeremy, taking his hands as if about to dance, tango-style. She leaned over him as far she could, which in her case, meant close to horizontal, so that he was forced to lean back with her.

And then she kissed him.

This wasn't one of those stage kisses in which lips are skillfully bypassed, nor was it one of those fond sisterly pecks on the cheek. No, it was an honest-to-goodness kiss that lasted far longer than a kiss ought, especially in public, the kind of kiss that makes you weak-kneed and gasping. Jeremy looked dazed as he returned to vertical, assisted by Drew. He wasn't used to women like Drew—or, I suppose, kisses like that.

"That's like a real *Casablanca* kiss," observed cornpone Todd. "You don't see many kisses like that anymore, do you?"

"No, you don't," Sky agreed.

# TWENTY

"There's all that water, that's why they need gondolas," my mother said. "But be careful. I heard from Selma Fine that there are more murders in Venice than in West Philadelphia."

"Hmm, I think she means Sicily, where the Mafia is, like in *The Godfather*. Venice is way north. I think most of the criminals stay down south, where they eat spaghetti. I don't think we'll meet them."

"It's Italy, isn't it? And they sided with Mussolini," she replied darkly.

In my mother's case, all roads did not lead to Rome but to Jews, and never with happy results. But books were a trustworthy diversion. "I've been reading Jan Morris, and Venice was a republic and Italy wasn't all one country. You remember, Sicily was a separate state like in *The Leopard*," I said.

"Lampedusa, a true genius, and no one knows him," she said, springing to life. "I hope Jeremy is reading all these books about Venice with you."

"He's probably read *Death in Venice*," I said, throwing her another bone.

My mother paused and then replied sharply, "*Death in Venice*, that's a strange choice if you ask me."

We reflected upon that novella's not-so-subtle homoerotic themes. Now, on top of my parents' other and all-too-numerous objections to Jeremy Levy, they would add repressed homosexual. "It's not one of his favorites. I meant, he probably read it in grad school like everyone else, and it's about Venice," I said.

"Wonderful. He read a book," she said. "Maybe he could read another, if it's not too much trouble, while he's in Hollywood writing garbage about people who kill."

"Right," I said, thinking of a comeback. "Well, he is paying for the entire trip, so I can't force him to read about it too. That's not fair."

"Bella, he's working and you're not."

"He is paying, that's what I just told you."

"He should pay!"

"Well, he is," I said, although truth was, we hadn't gone into the details of who did what, and what cost what. But since I had no money, I figured that he was paying.

"He has a good job and you are in school, studying who knows what, but no one's asking me. And anyway, you can come to Cape Cod with me and Daddy, and you don't have to pay for anything, even a crab sandwich—not that you ever eat, you are so thin, it's terrible."

"I do eat," I said, exhausted. Good thing that I hadn't mentioned the prospect of marrying Jeremy—I'd never hear the end of that one.

"Seriously, honey, it is exciting to go to Venice," she said. "I am happy for you."

My mother had never been to Europe, even once, except when she was born there—and that wasn't a good story. "I know you are, Mom," I said. "I'll send you lots of postcards."

Most years, I'd taken a week or two on Cape Cod with my parents at summer's end. By then, the crowds had thinned, and the Atlantic had warmed. My parents rented a house in a quiet town, nothing fancy. As far as vacations went, it was fine. I hadn't planned for anything better this year, especially since money was tight. I had been wrapped up in graduate school and the vocabulary study, and…Francois Morel.

All this is by way of explaining that I'd never given two thoughts to the issue of vacations—never, that is, until after Drew's flamboyant kiss. I tried to erase the memory of Jeremy's captivated smile. It gave me a pit in my stomach. I had no right to be jealous. Zero. But if feelings made sense, I guess that they wouldn't be feelings.

We left the restaurant without holding hands, not speaking the whole way home—a long walk, too. I was feeling foggy and tired of trying to read Jeremy's mind—I wasn't very good at it, either. Finally, I said, "Drew's attractive, isn't she?"

"Drew is just an actress who's playing herself," he said. "But what about you?"

I played dumb. "You already know who I am."

Jeremy looked at me straight in the eyes. "Is there someone else?"

"You know I love you," I said. That was true, and as for the other, I wasn't ready to name the feeling. "Jeremy, I am really tired. We need to get some sleep."

He kissed me. "Maybe we need to take a vacation, just a week or two alone. It's what we need. What do you think?"

I thought about how very married Francois was. I wasn't in that deep yet—a single kiss, even if it was all that I thought about, even when I tried not to. Escaping wasn't the worst solution: food, wine, song, anything to distract me. A holiday might be a cliché, but it might work. It was a worth a try.

I nodded "yes," trying not to cry—a bad habit of mine that I was determined to break, crying at unexpected moments. I couldn't speak yet, but I kept nodding and taking deep breaths, in and out, in and out, slowly and steadily. As long as I breathed, I wouldn't cry, and the worst part, I couldn't tell Jeremy why.

"Anywhere you want to go, anywhere is fine with me. Anywhere that makes you happy. Just say where and we'll go," he said.

And the morning after, I knew where I wanted to go—Venice.

Where I got the yen for Venice is impossible to say—it popped up from nowhere, as yens do. As a college student, I'd "done" the usual tour of Europe with my college roommate. We'd enjoyed cheap food, ugly hostels, and shared bathrooms, visiting the highlights, the big cities—London, Paris, Rome, and Florence—where, invariably, we bumped into old high school friends as though on a school trip. But we'd skipped Venice like a second-tier attraction—I think we chose Capri instead.

Venice wasn't a stranger, though. I knew it from movies—most of all, *Summertime*, with a spinsterish Katherine Hepburn and a tender Italian actor with liquid eyes—it was often on TV. I'd seen that Venice was a city of narrow canals, a city without cars, and a city with a beautiful open square where tourists flirted, where a grand church stood. A city where people fell in love. A city of over a hundred miniature islands, divided by canals and linked by bridges.

"Venice," I told him.

He repeated, humoring me, "Venice…OK, we can go to Venice."

"Venice is so romantic, don't you think? I mean, even the word lagoon is wonderful. It sounds magical, lagoon." I repeated the word about a dozen times—and he laughed and said, lagoon, lagoon, lagoon.

Our logistics quickly fell into place: our passports were in order, we found a flight for the following week, and we picked hotels from the *Frommer Guide, Europe on $10 a Day*, the cheapster's travel bible. No reason to spend more, I reasoned—I lived on less than $10 a day in Philly. That left time for me to become soaked in all matters Venetian—I memorized the names of bridges, streets, churches, palaces, battles, dates, paintings. I bought an Italian phrase book. Francois gave me one of his well-worn British guidebooks, Hugh Honour's *The Companion Guide to Venice.*

Francois wrote down a few must-sees: a Veronese church, Palazzo Labia, the tiny island of San Giorgio Maggiore. He said, "Venice is a strange city. Some people can't get over it and others just see dirty water."

"I'm already in love with Venice," I said. "Even if it vanished tomorrow, I'd be in love with it—it's sinking, it's disappearing into the sea, it's slowly dying. It's heartbreaking if you think about it. I can't help it, I am sentimental."

"So am I," he said.

I placed a tiny faint B on his calendar, on the date when I'd return. Not that he needed a reminder. But even so, he'd look at it.

# TWENTY ONE

We hit Venice in the peak tourist season: early July. That pleased me—Venice was meant for sightseeing. It had always been a city on parade, a city of theatrical display. I didn't want an empty Square, I wanted throngs of visitors, in bright sunlight or mist, framed by twisted shapes, pigeons flying above. I'd had my fill of solitary parks in Philadelphia where no one walked except for the old or the homeless.

There was a day or two of churches and art and food, and the uncanny light of Venice. The Venetians seemed poised for adventure, but elegant. I made a note to buy many gaily colored silk scarves when I could afford them.

But Jeremy and I walked on eggshells.

Partly, it was the fault of our hotel, described in the guidebook as "delightfully old-fashioned." Our tiny ("perfectly comfortable") room consisted of one smallish bed, one dilapidated dresser, and an aging leaky bathroom. It was stuffy and hot, and if we dared to open a window, hostile flies swarmed in. Through paper-thin walls, we could hear whispers, shuffling, running water, loud flushing, and every bedspring's motion. And if anything can get one out of the mood, it's the moaning of fellow ("friendly") guests who are in the mood. It made one nostalgic for the charms of a Holiday Inn.

"Frommer never visited this place," Jeremy observed as he swatted another fly.

It was too late to find another hotel, but Venice was Venice, and I didn't care.

It might have been our third day when we walked across the small bridge that Byron named the Bridge of Sighs, another fact that I learned from my *Companion Guide*. Legend had it that lovers kissing under the bridge at sunset, when the bells chimed, would be granted eternal bliss. Standing there, as if by design, was a young man who looked beamed in from a Renaissance portrait—clear light eyes, aquiline nose, a feminine, sultry mouth, and rather dandyish outfit. He posed for another man—his lover, I guessed—and smiled at me, daring me not to admire him. I returned his crooked smile, in appreciation of the pleasure of having seen him where he belonged, on this miracle of a bridge at sunset. And I watched them stroll off, their slender figures dissolving into an archway, like a painting I had yet to see.

"How perfect on the Bridge of Sighs," I said. "This is the last view that prisoners had before they were locked up. They sighed at how beautiful Venice looked. You can see how the light hits the lagoon at the time of day. Isn't it wonderful?"

"I'd rather see a sunset at the Grand Canyon," Jeremy said, in a bored voice.

Like a reprimand, the famed bells rang, all of them—and if we kissed now, we might be granted eternal bliss. A magical instant, and Jeremy thought only of Arizona.

I wanted to scream. Yes! It's a terrific canyon that everyone visits, and it's more crowded than Venice. It has a gift shop that sells T-shirts, cheesy key chains, corny postcards of sunrises, and a restaurant that was worse than bad. Traffic is god-awful getting there, and unless you start your hike by 5 a.m., you meet more people on the trails than in a Manhattan subway, plus you compete with donkeys and flies. Besides, Arizona's heat could kill anyone, and Venice was a breezy 80 degrees—and we were in Venice, a city where history was made.

I said, "These bells have rung for centuries: Each one's different and we're here listening to them, the same bells, the same chimes. Doesn't that mean anything to you?"

"I know," he said in a pained voice, "but I'm tired of cities."

I waited until the melodious chimes ended. There was a faint echo and the sounds hung in the air, like ancient memories. The city seemed to stop. Everyone held their breath to listen to the last echo—everyone except Jeremy, who saw only limestone and muddy water.

"We are in Venice and you'd like to be hiking in Arizona? Is that what you are saying?" I asked.

"Or on a beach," he said, as if that improved the situation.

"A beach? You would like to be on a beach?"

"Sure, a beach would be fine."

"No one forced you to come, Jeremy. You don't have to look so long-suffering."

He gave me one of his looks and said, "I did it for you."

"This is like me going to a Yankees game, let's say the playoffs, and all I did was go on about some museum. But I wouldn't do that because I wouldn't want to spoil it because I know how much you love the Yankees. So I'd have a beer and a hot dog, and try and enjoy the game, which by the way, I would, because we'd be outside and together and why not enjoy it as long as I'm there? That's what I would do, and this, *this* is what you do."

"I get the point. I'll be quiet."

"But if you're quiet..." I said, close to tears. And then I was crying, uncontrollably, even though I had promised myself that I wouldn't, not under any circumstances.

"I'm not some big mystery. If I don't speak, you're wondering what I'm thinking, but I don't really have any secrets. I wish we were in a decent hotel with air-conditioning and we weren't in a city."

"Not here, you mean," I said. "But we are here, that's the point. This is where we are."

"Bella, please," he said. "Don't turn this into something it's not."

We were alone on the Bridge of Sighs, with the clear blue skies of Venice above us, a blue that I'd thought was invented by Bellini, but was in fact the sky's true color. A golden light hit the surface of the lagoon, and I felt the anguish of the prisoners' final view, and I wondered which alley the two young men had drifted into. But all that Jeremy saw was dirty brown water, and old crumbling buildings—or maybe, he was daydreaming about the Yankees.

Francois Morel's words returned to me: Not everyone understands Venice.

I said, "Go back to the hotel and try to get some sleep or read. I'll meet you later for dinner—there's more I want to see, and I promise I won't be long."

"We're in a foreign country," he said. "I don't want you to get lost."

"We're not in a wilderness, we're in Venice," I said. "Actually, believe it or not, I know where I am. Really, Jeremy, I know exactly where I am."

He gave me a brief troubled kiss and said, "OK, but don't be late."

I confidently headed toward the Dorsoduro district to find one of the "must-sees" on Francois's list, the small sixteenth-century church of San Sebastian, whose interiors were painted by Veronese and which houses his tomb. At that hour, it was empty and silent, and I heard the echo of my footsteps. I had it all to myself. At least if I burst into tears, no one would see me.

Its ceilings glowed with lush images of men and women, alive and happy, in satin and silk. The whole church reflected a sense of earthly joy, worldly pleasures, fleeting and impossibly beautiful. I knew that Veronese had been a young man when he painted it, and it had the freshness of youth, the impetuousness—even with his own tomb there. I sat for a while, imprinting the images in my memory so I could take them home.

Upon leaving, I met a well-dressed older man emerging from the shadows—Venice has sharp corners that produce that effect. It might have been the hour of the day or my state of mind, but he seemed ghostly. He wore a silk ascot and a beret, both black.

"Veronese," I heard him say.

In refined English, he told me that the church was impoverished, in need of restoration, its survival threatened by earthquakes and rising water.

"It's criminal that something so beautiful is forgotten," I told him.

He smiled, "You won't forget it."

"Never," I said.

On the way back to the hotel, I stopped at one of those newsstands that sold postcards and stamps. I settled for a picture of the Bridge of Sighs. On it I wrote, "I'm in love," and nothing else except his address. My postcard might arrive in Philadelphia after I did. Even so, I slipped it into a mailbox.

I needed to tell someone how I felt.

# TWENTY TWO

Miraculously, Sky and Jeremy's drafts for *Scared Jim* improved. But Sky was still on the fence about the ending, and I guess that's why he called me. Sky never slept, from what I could tell, since it was seven in the morning my time, four his, and he was wide awake.

"This lizard thing, I don't know," he said. "What do you think?"

"The lizard, well, it's just a lizard. I think a super-cool girlfriend should rescue Jim at the end after he falls into the magic well. She could have psychic powers, which, between you and me, I think all girlfriends should possess," I said.

"A girl with superpowers…maybe someone like Drew Hayworth."

I wasn't surprised. Drew Hayworth certainly had powers, as far as men were concerned. Sky had been wowed by her leggy dancing in *Timid Jim: The Musical*—I was, too. But I couldn't help suspecting that what tipped the scales for Sky was her sultry tango with Jeremy. That kiss was hard to forget, in a sickening way, like devil's food cake after a heavy dinner.

"She is sexy," I said.

"Make that very," he said, and next thing I knew, Drew was in the cast.

That's how Sky Lowe made decisions, amidst the ever-looming deadlines and never-ending frenzy of filmmaking. And *Scared Jim* got finished—with, as Sky had promised me, Jeremy as writer.

With Sky's media savvy, he had arranged the premiere at a museum in New York—to lend the event a gravitas that most "teen pics" lacked. By that time, it had slowly cycled through the hipper film festivals like Telluride, picking up a flurry of awards.

Sky said, "I've booked rooms at the Waldorf. Why don't you come? Natasha can drive you from Philly."

"I am dying to go, I admit it. I've never been close to a real premiere. But I haven't seen Jeremy since we got back from Italy. It could get awkward, especially since I changed his ending."

"My ending," Sky shot back. "Not his ending."

"Well, he isn't going to be thrilled to see me."

"Let Jeremy worry about Jeremy," he said. "I know you like to dress up, this is your chance."

I pictured myself in dark maroon lipstick, shiny rhinestone clip earrings—and, against my better instincts, I was curious to see Jeremy. "If you put it that way," I said. "It might be my last chance to go to a real premiere with real movie stars."

Then I spent the next week or so driving myself crazy about what to wear. I tried on dress and after dress, and called my mother to describe, in minute detail, the virtues and defects of each. My mother's visual memory included every garment I'd ever worn, including many horrors I tried my best to forget.

"Wear your new Hattie Carnegie," was her verdict. "It's 1950s and no one will be wearing anything like that." It was navy blue silk organza, a stiff wide princess-like skirt with tiny jet-black buttons up the front—ultra-prim, Grace Kelly-elegant, defiantly vintage.

All's well that ends well, I thought as I entered the austere lobby of MOMA. It was a great dress, even against the stiff competition. I'd never seen so many perfect looking women in one place—that is, alive, breathing, and talking. It was as though every smile were Photoshopped. By contrast, the actors looked deliberately unkempt, with creased, shrunken jackets and thick retro eyeglasses, as if freshly sprung from an Actor's Studio

Workshop. As for Sky, he was himself—a little flabbier after grueling months of post-production.

The Parents Lowenstein were much as I expected—the urbane New York couple. Pa Lowenstein resembled Sky—tallish, curly hair, although his was grey, with lively hazel eyes that promised a sense of fun. Ma was a small friendly-looking woman who wore gigantic silver jewelry with abstract shapes, the type that artists sign. I figured that she'd bought her kimono-style jacket on some excursion to Tokyo or Hong Kong.

Mr. L. informed me, "Our son, Teddy, teaches physics at Caltech. He's received the Wolf Prize, and he'll probably win the Nobel. Natasha's won a MacArthur Genius Grant. I guess it's Sky's turn."

Natasha wore an avant-garde dress of frightening severity, hair cut shorter than a boy's. She gave her head a few clarifying shakes and said, "Sky doesn't need a prize to get rich."

"I think he will win an Oscar," I assured Mr. L.

Mrs. L. confided in hushed tones, "I hope it's not one of those movies where everyone mumbles. Last film I could hardly follow a thing."

"Who can understand?" protested Mr. L. as if speaking of Biblical events. "All these men screaming and buildings exploding, it doesn't make any sense." He looked at me, shaking his head grimly.

I said, "Teens don't expect the linear stories that we grew up with. They're looking for unpredictability and novelty, like a game. It's what I study."

"So you study stories and Natasha studies how taxi drivers talk," remarked Mrs. L. drily. "People study everything these days." She blinked as if she were overwhelmed at the newfangled world. I imagine that in Ma Lowenstein's youth, it was Byron or mathematics, with little in between.

Sky came over and put his arms around me and Mrs. L. "Yes, it's a *Brave New World.* This is the Bella I mentioned, the one who showed me the stories."

"Bella, I remember," said the Missus.

Natasha poked her mother, and said emphatically, "When you go away, Bella could mind the cat for you. She misses New York."

"I do love cats," I said, "the animal type, not the musical."

"A fellow cat lover," said Mr. L. with surprising sweetness. "So you're Natasha's student and you find Sky his stories. You're a Renaissance woman, I think."

My old self would have spilled the beans to kind Mr. L.: that the stories had been written by my boyfriend who wasn't a boyfriend anymore, not even a friend, and who wasn't speaking to me.

My new self said quietly, "I didn't do much. It was a favor for a friend."

"Speaking of the devil," murmured Sky to me. "I should have mentioned he's here with Drew."

"He's allowed to have a date," I said as I checked them out—she in a skintight red dress that plunged without regard, and Jeremy absurdly handsome in a tux. I wondered what he thought of her seminude state. Jeremy never liked low necklines.

Sky gave me a funny look and said, "A date, right." We advanced toward them.

Jeremy managed a twisted smile, more of a grimace. But Drew greeted me like a long-lost relative. "Bella, you're here! That is so amazing! You are the reason that I am here and now you are here. We are both here, together. It's beautiful." She miled, wide-eyed, like a Moonie holding a tin cup at the airport.

It was tiring keeping track of Drew's slippery personae, from diehard Yankees fan to flirty waitress to New Age Starlet. She morphed with the moment. It might be an occupational hazard with actresses—faking kept them in shape, like training for thespians. I said, "You belong here, and I really don't."

"You do," said Jeremy with a new polish that he must have acquired in Hollywood, of all places. "That's a very nice dress, Bella."

I crowed inwardly and made a note to tell my mother. "Thank you. And it's good to see both of you."

Drew embraced me with a Hollywood hug that managed to avoid mussing her hairdo or conveying a shred of genuine affection—as though she were hugging an old lady in a mayoral campaign. Her broad shoulders did have the effect of making me feel frail, if not elderly—with the added artillery of her high heels, Drew had a good five inches on me.

"Yes, you are SO amazing!" she chirped insanely. "I love you, I do! You are such a good person and so accepting!"

Drew Hayworth had never been more than a casual acquaintance. I could not say that I loved her. Truth was, I was debating whether I liked her. At the moment, I leaned toward the "not like" column, at least in her most recent Hollywood incarnation. As for Jeremy and me, love was out of the question on that front as well. Well, maybe that counted as accepting—but who knew, with a woman like Drew?

Sky said, "Drew, you should meet some people." He rattled off a few luminaries whose first names surely quickened Drew's pulse and steered her in their direction. That left me alone with Jeremy, or relatively alone—we were surrounded by semi-naked women who sported more diamonds than fabric.

"Ill met by moonlight, Jeremy," I said. "It's been ages…maybe…"

"Two years," he said listlessly.

Jeremy hated small talk, and this was the worst kind. This was filler, what you say when you have nothing left to say, or you can't say what you want to.

"That seems like ages," I replied, nervously. "I left you a message on your last birthday. I guess you didn't want to hear from me."

"No, I didn't," he said. "It took a while to…"

He didn't finish his sentence. I wondered what took a while, for him to stop hating me or stop loving me. Either way, happy wasn't what he felt when he heard my message—it had been a blunder. Even cards from ex-girlfriends are an atrocious idea with words like "merry" and "joyous." Ex-girlfriends should know better.

I said, "The script's yours, give or take a few scenes and the ending."

Jeremy said, "A Sky Lowe movie is a Sky Lowe movie. Your ending was a good idea. That's how we got Drew."

I caught Drew laughing at some apparent hilarity in the corner of the room. I was fascinated how her skimpy dress stayed vertical—maybe she taped it?

I was tired of small talk as well. "I was thinking, maybe we could meet for coffee tomorrow, if you want to, if you're free."

"Not exactly," said Jeremy, studying his shoes intently, as was his habit in times of discomfort. "Drew's parents are in town this weekend."

Drew, parents, plans—they were a real couple. Sky had never mentioned it. He probably assumed that their romance would fall apart post-production as movie flings often do: the fiery heat of the moment, chilled when the film wraps. But I could have told Sky, Jeremy did not have flings. He wasn't a casual guy. He was the other kind, the kind who held on for life.

"You and Drew," I said as if I were in a spelling bee and handed one of those impossible words.

"We've been living together for a year." He spoke like a teacher who wanted to make sure I got the point.

Two years since our breakup, minus one living with Drew. He hadn't waited long, had he? Not that I'd wanted him to enter a monastery and make buckwheat honey, but still, a year of mourning would have been intensely gratifying. But men like Jeremy don't stay single for long. Women are not that lunatic, despite what all those TV talk shows say.

"I guess you're in Santa Monica?" I asked. I pictured a bikini-clad Drew playing beach volleyball. Come to think of it, I did not like Drew. In fact, I sort of loathed her in all of her varied incarnations, New Age or flirty or even Yankees fan.

"No, we're here. We were tired of L.A. and the real estate market was good. Drew's good at stuff like that."

I thought of the Bard's line, that fortune brings in some boats that are not steered. I forget why I'd bothered to memorize it though. I said, "So everything worked out."

Jeremy looked momentarily stunned. "You're impossible," he said, and I leaned over and brushed my lips against his cheek, just barely, and whispered, "I know, I know." He tasted salty, the way he always did.

After a while, he said, "You're seeing someone?"

By now, I had invented a boyfriend to throw people off track. "Yes, Larry was supposed to come tonight, but he travels, you know, to other countries. He flies a lot, he's a frequent flyer."

"He doesn't sail," he deadpanned.

"Not professionally," I giggled. "Jeremy, it sounds corny, but I want you to be really, really happy. Drew likes the Yankees, she plays softball and tennis and I can't even run or jog even. I can walk, though."

"Yes, you can walk," he said with a faint smile. "You're wearing glasses."

"I'm getting used to them. I squeaked by the driving test, just barely, and finally I broke down and bought glasses. I couldn't handle contacts. You know me, I'd lose them. Funny thing is, I was walking around all those years not seeing. I got used to things being blurry. I thought the world was blurry or fuzzy. Anyway, I love the whole vision thing—all these things in the distance, details, like Drew over there, I can see her, crystal-clear."

He adjusted the frames ever so slightly upwards. "There."

"So you think I look okay in them?"

He studied me mock-seriously and said, "I like them a lot."

"If you like them…" I said. I didn't have to finish the thought, not for him.

"I do," he said. "Drew and I went back to Venice last year for the film festival. It was great. I owe you an apology for spoiling it."

We looked at one another, straight in the eye, unflinching. I thought back to our first kiss outside my apartment, how it had shocked me with its force. I hadn't been prepared for how unprotected it was. I hadn't expected that. For one split second, I wanted to tell him the truth about Francois Morel. He deserved that much—I owed him that much.

But all I said was, "I think tomorrow isn't such a great idea."

And then Sky and Drew returned, and we all entered the MOMA screening room. Sky insisted on sitting in the back row, so he could gauge the audience response. Drew and Jeremy sat further toward the front, her head on his shoulder. Not far behind them were Sky's parents, holding hands. I saw Mrs. L. sneak her curly-haired husband a kiss. All these couples and I wasn't part of one. I didn't mind being single, but sometimes I forgot that's what I was. Married boyfriends didn't count.

*Scared Jim* was, by turns, fantastic, scary, and funny. The young hero fell into gigantic battles, secret wells and tunnels and choppy seas, leaping from reality to fantastic dreams—and all to the pulse of hypnotic techno-music. For two hours, I was as immersed as anyone in the audience—despite the fact that I had read countless drafts of the screenplay, tested storyboards, and even created the movie's ending. None of it mattered. I gasped as if it were all brand new and fresh.

And on top of all of that, Sky had snuck in a producer's credit for me—and there was my name, in big letters!

"It's even better than *Kill More or Die!*," I said to Sky. "Like when the well turned into the ocean, that was great! It was amazing! I can't believe what you did, Sky."

"Hey, don't look so shocked, I do this for a living. Movies don't happen by accident. People make them, people like you and me. That's how films get made, Bella."

"I know, that is what is so incredible. I mean, people make great movies like this, plus they get paid for it. I mean, people like you make movies."

"Or you," he said quietly.

"Me?" I asked.

"Yes, people like you. Just think about it, that's all I'm asking."

# TWENTY THREE

Next morning, I visited Sue and Ben's now-booming establishment: "Fast Hair." There were neon-colored Fast Hair T-shirts, Fast Hair shampoos and conditioners, Fast Hair blow dryers and Fast Hair mugs, each with a darling face of a blue-eyed, pink-cheeked baby. A dozen twenty-something hairdressers in Fast Hair uniform, young women sporting miniskirts and skinny tank tops, all of it a far cry from Ben's former shabby chic.

The former Sue Olinsky, now Sue Grace, graciously handed me a Fast Hair mug. "I tell Ben, if he hadn't married me, he'd be cutting hair at ninety. Now we've got three shops and we're opening next year in the Hamptons," she laughed. "But enough about Fast Hair, I want to hear everything about the premiere, starting from the top, which is Jeremy. I'm still mad that he didn't come to the wedding."

"I had broken up with him," I said weakly. I figured that counted for something.

"No excuse," said Sue, disproving that particular hypothesis. "Go on."

"The premiere was amazing. But seeing Jeremy was somewhere between horrible and miserable. He showed up with Drew of all people, who's starring in the movie. She's the one Ben used to date before you—the pretty waitress who was an actress."

"Ben dated a lot of those," said Sue sarcastically.

"So I had one of those Pavlovian responses like with the dog and the bell when I saw him. One look at Jeremy, I feel fat and insecure." I might have added that Francois Morel made me feel slender and gorgeous, but naturally, no one knew about him—just as well, since Sue would have lectured me.

Sue's eyes squinted, like Dr. Joyce Brothers. "You were never fat. I was fat." She roared with laughter at the memory of her former chunkiness.

"Curvaceous," said Ben, with a wink. Sue had nabbed one sexy guy when she got Ben.

"Fat's a state of mind," I explained, half joking. "You see, physically, I am thin, so that's one data point. But psychologically, it's like there's a fat me waiting to break out of the thin me. Like today, I'm maybe a pound away from fat…maybe two."

Ben offered me a Lorna Doone—Fast Hair offered the buttery pleasures, on paper plates, along with herbal tea. "Twenty is more like it," he said sympathetically.

I took one of the forty-calorie treats. "Thanks. Anyway, it was weird learning about Jeremy and Drew…"

"About them getting married," said Ben, as though following my train of thought rather than derailing it.

I grabbed another Lorna Doone, only half-believing him. I'd hidden the truth from Jeremy, but I assumed that he was honest with me. He had no reason to be, though, did he?

Sue shot Ben a dark look. "Men," she snorted. "I wonder if they're even semi-intelligent." To me, she said, "What can you do? An inferior species. Anyway, that's the press that Drew's releasing. Did you notice a ring?"

"There were so many diamonds that I wouldn't have noticed. It was kind of an ocean of large gemstones."

"Rented," said Sue dismissively. She prepared a mint tea for me, two sugars.

"Drew definitely has a ring," said Ben, "and a date. She's booked the stylists here. I'm sorry if you didn't know."

"Oh," I said, sipping my herbal tea.

"Jeremy never deserved you in the first place. First you weren't speaking, then you were, then he was throwing out your dresses, and really, he's a total pain," said Sue. "But I want to hear about Sky Lowe. He's kind of cute, like a SoHo teddy bear."

"Forget teddy bears, it is not like that," I said. "Sky has a development company, downtown in TriBeCa. Now, he's thinking bigger, developing movies for other directors, TV. He wants me to work with him to scout material, guide projects, it's all…"

"Pie in the *Sky*," she quipped, tickled by her own wordplay. "Seriously, what's the problem? You could be like Faye Dunaway in *Network*."

I pictured myself as the overambitious, oversexed executive—not a happy vision, except for the attractive pencil skirts. But before I could express my doubts, Sue was calculating the cost of moving, rents in Manhattan, Brooklyn, Queens, and even Hoboken, daily living expenses, city and state taxes, bus, subway and taxi fares, with her uncanny spreadsheet precision. She passed me a number, started to instruct me on the art of negotiating.

"Not so fast," I replied. "I might not be ready."

Sue snorted. "I'm not ready either. Who is ever ready?" Seeing my confusion, she said, "Bella, you are the least observant person on the planet. Don't you ever notice anything?"

Sue's hair was a few shades lighter, but it was still long. I said, "I do. You have this whole new salon with all this stuff. And you have these Fast Hair mugs, which are great, but why is there a baby on them? It's a cute baby, too."

Sue said, "You're getting close. Keep going."

"Oh, you're opening a salon for kids! That's a truly fantastic concept," I said.

"No, we are not," said Sue, giving me one of her fresh-from-Bellevue looks.

I inspected the cartoon baby for further clues.

"Try again," she said. "This isn't a trick question. Love, marriage, what comes next?"

Ben hummed a strain of "Makin' Whoopee" and smiled—a sweet, patient smile, too.

Of course, love, marriage, and family.

I thought of the party when I noticed Sue's engagement ring. She had used the word "jealous." The feel of the word had lingered. It took me a while to understand why. Sue lived in a world of love, marriage, and then family—engagements, weddings, anniversaries, holidays, birthdays, and, yes, kids and grandkids, all flowing in the right order. She expected that; I hadn't. That's what it meant: expectant.

I said, "I'm a moron. You two will be the best parents ever. Your kids will be really lucky."

"If they look like Ben," said Sue.

# TWENTY FOUR

"I can't believe that Natasha roped me into teaching the summer session. It's crazy that parents pay jillions of dollars and their kids get taught by me," I said.

In our office, Jessica sipped her green tea, unperturbed—she and my fellow doctoral candidates had been teaching for years. "When did millions become jillions or zillions?" Her specialty was predicting when slang became mainstream, especially words that travelled the path from negative to positive (like the ever-changing "queer").

Jessica's star was rising. She churned out articles and was quoted in journals and at conferences. She had adopted a sexy schoolgirl style: clunky black lace-ups, tweed miniskirts, crisp white oxford shirts, her hair cut with bangs.

"1940s, Damon Runyan, maybe," I said. "Depression slang."

"Damon Runyan, hmm," she said. "How do you know all these writers?"

"I read," I replied.

"I read," she reminded me sternly. She waved at a tall, forbidding stack of academic journals and books. The journals were arranged chronologically and the books alphabetized; within each letter, Jessica kept her alphabetical system going. Maintaining their correct order seemed like hard work, but that was Jessica.

"I mean reading for fun. Damon Runyan is funny. You know, *Guys and Dolls?*"

She fingered the spines, her brow wrinkling. "I don't have time," she said, but not sadly. It was a fact of academic life.

Our exchange once might have depressed me. We were, after all, in the halls of higher education with an enormous library, actually many different, wonderful libraries. But the beleaguered grad students never read for anything close to pleasure. Damon Runyan might have been a Filipino author for all they knew, although, if he had written in Tagalog, his lively gangsters would end up in a dry footnote.

"If Natasha says you can do it, you can," Jessica said, and as usual, said the name Natasha with a special reverence.

I hoped, or prayed, that I didn't look as slack-jawed when I talked about Francois. "How do I do this without making a fool of myself?"

"Just follow the syllabus and read from your notes."

"That sounds boring," I said hesitantly.

"Well, embrace your inner boring," Jessica said.

I taught in a smallish dismal room that overlooked a pleasant square courtyard, which in summer looked leafy-green and shaded. My students gazed upon it with longing, presumably envying all those lucky souls who were not stuck listening to me. The ten or so undergraduates in my section were pre-law, pre-med, or Wharton-bound, sharp as tacks. They had chosen Codes and Modes as an easy elective to satisfy their "other" requirement. Compared to organic chemistry, this course should have been a snap—no formulas to memorize, nothing complex.

But suffice it to say, if I had taught Thomas Edison, the world would be lit by candles.

"Yes, semiotics…linguistics studies words and language, while semiotics studies signs, symbols, and meaning," I recited from my file card. But I found the next file card mysteriously blank, so I improvised, "Things can be just things like a hamburger, which is food you eat, or you can eat if you want to. But a hamburger has lots of cultural and social and economic and even artistic significance, like if you hear about someone giving a party and serving hamburgers, you know it's a certain kind of party. It's probably not a fancy party, maybe more casual like a frat party. So, it's not just food. It's a cultural icon."

A quick flip through my colored file cards revealed that they were all blank. I had carried the wrong stack. After staying up half of the night preparing, I was empty-handed.

I struggled for my next thought, as through a glass darkly. "If you are a serious semiotician like Saussure, everything is a sign of something. Signs mean different things to different people. Like vegetarians don't eat hamburgers. Maybe that is not the greatest example."

"I don't think Russians eat hamburgers. It's against their religion," volunteered a fair-haired boy with pale wild eyes. I could never recall his name, despite his remarkable, nay, astounding, genius for going off-track.

"I thought the Russians didn't have a religion," muttered someone from the back of the room. "They're all…atheists and communists."

"They're not true communists anymore," said the fair-haired boy bitterly. He wrote something in what looked like a personal diary. His eyes darted furtively, as if there were spies lurking in the classroom.

I nodded and attempted to retrieve the semblance of my original lecture—which had been a long list of proper names and meaningless jargon.

"We can find symbols in everything, even if it seems trivial and something that most people don't think about. For example, Russians don't think about hamburgers, or maybe they don't think about them."

I stopped there. The Russian theme had me astray. Russians ate foods like borscht and caviar and blini. They drank gallons of vodka and sang melancholy ballads. What was my point? I could write something on the blackboard—but what?

"Unless they're in semiotics," yawned a cute guy whose name was Jeff. He wore the same alligator polo shirts that Jeremy had. "Before I took this course, believe me, I never thought about hamburgers except when I wanted one rare. But hey, I'm pre-med."

"That Peirce guy is worse. He is a total lunatic," said Jill, who, I could tell, liked Jeff—but he hadn't noticed her at all, which I found far more intriguing than either loony Peirce or obscure Saussure, since Jeff, from what I could tell, yearned for a nice sweet girlfriend and well-dressed Jill seemed ideal if he only noticed, which as it happened, was under my power to control.

I said, "Jeff, what would you say about Peirce? Jill here thinks he's a lunatic."

"I'd say Jill and I have something in common," laughed Jeff, which caused Jill to blush, much to my delight.

"You're both sort of right. Peirce was a Sad Sack," I said, veering wildly off the script. "He never held a real job, and everyone more or less thought he was nuts."

The kids looked as if I had pulled the spring on the Jack-in-the-Box.

I added, "And the poor guy died broke."

Jeff said, gleefully, "Ha! I knew it. Guys like him always die broke."

The class broke into peals of violent laughter. I had amused them, although inadvertently. Next time, I could try slipping on a banana peel or speaking in tongues.

"It's pathetic," said Jill. "You see he was crazy, so that's why he couldn't write clearly and it's kind of crazy-talk. I'm used to history and stuff that is logical, like the Napoleonic Wars, stuff that makes sense."

"Hmm, Napoleon died alone. Waterloo wasn't exactly logical," I said, mildly.

"Compared to Peirce, it was," she grumbled. Jeff gave an approving nod.

Jeff yawned and said, "So we're getting tested on Peirce, too, not just Saussure?"

The kids gazed at me in a helpless stupor. I didn't blame them. They would, or so I felt, make fine suburban doctors and lawyers without learning about the likes of Ferdinand de Saussure and his maniacal penchant for signs.

I shrugged apologetically. Defeated, they picked up their books. But as they left, I noticed Jill and Jeff whispering together. At least I was good for something, if not the instruction of semiotics—besides, as soon as the final exam ended, the nouns and jargon of Codes and Modes would fly away like bits of trash on a windy day.

I marched into Natasha's office, where I found her petting her large Great Dane and readying to leave school. I burst out, "I can't do this, Natasha, it's a disaster."

"Walk with me. Leo's restless, aren't you Leo? We can walk home together…I didn't drive today." Her Great Dane looked up at her, lovingly.

"It's bad," I said. "It's not because I'm not working hard. I'm working until early in the morning, but I'm not getting anywhere."

"Well, your students like you," she said. "They say you're funny."

"Because I went easy on the midterms," I said. "I'm into a Zen process, grading-wise. Jessica thinks I'm a marshmallow, and she's right."

"Jessica could stand a little more Zen," said Natasha, pulling Leo along. "Has she talked to you about what's going on?"

"No," I said. "But I see stuff. Some student threw a fit the other day—strange girl. She wouldn't leave. She sat there, staring a long time. It felt wrong."

"Did you hear what they said?" Natasha asked.

"I was transcribing, so no, I didn't try to hear. But the student started pounding her fists on Jessica's desk. It got ugly. Jessica wouldn't talk about it."

"Hmm," said Natasha, looking worried.

Walking home, we passed over the wide Schuylkill and saw Philadelphia's skyline on the other side. Once upon a time, the city respected a gentleman's agreement not to build higher than the figure of William Penn atop City Hall. It wasn't a law, but everyone treated it that way—and that lent Center City an intimacy, even a certain gracefulness. But slowly, the skyline was being pulled upward. Philadelphia would soon be an ordinary American city of skyscrapers and fast food, glass, and steel.

I said, "The way the city is going, no one's going to able to see the statue of William Penn from where we are. History's being erased."

"Cities change," she said casually and then added with equal lightness, "Bella, if you really don't want to teach, you have other options."

"Where?" I asked.

"Well, research for one. Francois thinks you'd be a strong candidate for that new center at Princeton," she said. "When he's back, he'll tell you more about it."

Up to that very second, I had imagined—or deluded myself—that Natasha had no clue about me and Francois, that it was a secret. Now I knew better.

"There's no reason to think that my research would be a good fit."

"I wouldn't worry about that," she said.

# TWENTY FIVE

Teaching was bad enough, but delivering the final grades was painful. Students argued, cajoled, wheedled, whined, and if all else failed, sobbed. It was like watching like the final stages of grief in slow motion. My last student of the long morning was a puffy-eyed Jill. She pointed to an exam question that she had boldly circled with a red magic marker.

"You asked us to name an American symbol. I said liberty," she said.

"But liberty isn't a symbol," I said delicately. "Other things can be a symbol of liberty, right? The Statue of Liberty is a symbol, or the Liberty Bell." I stopped myself since I could see Jill light up, and not with the flame of liberty.

"Liberty Bell! I forgot the 'Bell' because I got distracted," she said. "I get this almost disability when I'm upset, which I was because you know, I was dating…someone…and it didn't work out." Jill gave a few ladylike sniffles and removed a package of Kleenex from her brand-new Coach bag. She must have gone shopping to console herself.

"I'm sorry," I said. Secretly, I was dying to hear about her breakup with Jeff. But that was off-limits.

Jessica Tang muttered, "At least her grandmother didn't die. We had a lot of dead grannies this week."

"That is not funny," said Jill, enraged. "I love my grandmother!"

"She didn't mean it," I said to Jill, but not quickly enough.

"I did," said Jessica with a bitter, humorless smile.

I felt like bopping Jessica on the head and screaming, "Hello!" but I feared no one was home. Something in the process of earning a PhD deprived people of sanity.

Later, I said to Jessica, "These kids are sensitive, you need to be careful."

"Who writes liberty instead of Liberty Bell? Pathetic. And you sound even more pathetic, listening to these lame excuses and pretending to believe them. Grades are already so inflated that it's a joke—please."

I tried to interject a light touch: "Look, let's say I'm on my deathbed. I'm old and I am dying, obviously. My life is flashing by me—all of my favorite movies, everything I love."

"People do not remember their favorite movies on their deathbed," said Jessica.

"It's my deathbed, I can do what I like. Anyway, there I am, looking back and what have you. Am I going to say, 'Oh no! I gave too many As!' I don't think so, Jess. I'll say, 'I should have given even more As!' You know, T.S. Elliot gave everyone an A just for showing up. And I am not a major Twentieth Century poet who wrote 'I can show you fear in a handful of dust.'"

I hadn't expected her to fall on the floor in hysterics, but I had hoped for more than a grumpy sigh. "I don't get you."

"I don't get me either, so why should you? Everything that seems simple turns out not to be simple. Nothing is simple, or social scientists wouldn't have anything to study, would they?"

"That's Francois Morel talking," she said. "I'll be back."

She stomped out of the office, Doc Martens first.

I left the door open. In summer, the building was mostly empty. I was transcribing the children's interviews, my headset on. It was slow-going, sort of like knitting, or what I thought knitting was like. I had worked through a fire drill once and the other students laughed about it. But that's how I worked best—I blocked everything out.

All of which must explain how I failed to notice when someone entered. The sickeningly sweet perfume alerted me: one of those musky heavy scents. I turned around and saw the student who had thrown a fit with Jessica. She wore a Brooks Brothers-style blazer, white pants, an expensive silk scarf. She stood in front of Jessica's desk.

"I hope I didn't frighten you," she said with an odd smile, implying that her hopes were in the opposite direction. I pictured her shouting at a frightened waiter in a fancy restaurant, sending her steak back: too rare, too well done, too hot, too cold, and where was her martini, anyway?

I marched over to Jessica's desk. "You are?" I asked.

"Sally Ruder," she said, as if I were a clerk. I imagine that's how many undergrads viewed us: they were paying clients, teachers were hired hands. It was a fair view of the relationship.

"Sally, this isn't a public library," I said.

"Of course not," she replied, all Lady Bountiful. "This morning, when I left my meeting with Jessica Tang, I realized that I'd left something behind."

Jessica's desk had mounds of computer printouts, articles-in-process, letters to editors, academic journals, newspaper clippings, all in tidy, orderly stacks. And on top of one mound, an exam from the previous semester. Even an easy grader like me knew there was an underground market selling old exams. A lucrative one, too. But why was Jessica looking at an older test?

"You need to leave now, Sally."

She gazed at me as though I were a flea. Her eyes were blue, but a milky blue, that seemed to look past me, almost as if she were blind.

"Now," I said.

She continued to stare at me, which felt worse than if she had screamed. I didn't know what was in her handbag—tear gas?

In theory, I could call "security," since, somewhere in our building, a kindly elderly man slumbered or ate powdered donuts. It was like having a sweet guard puppy instead of a Doberman. As to his whereabouts, I had no clue. Leaving milky-eyed Sally alone was not an option—but neither was staying with her. She was a loaded cannon.

Jessica returned with coffee, and for a second, I thought Sally might attack her. But Sally marched out, heels clicking loudly, slowly, deliberately. I checked that the hall was empty before I shut the door.

"What the hell is going on?" I asked.

# TWENTY SIX

While Francois was in Tokyo, I received a postcard every afternoon: Mount Fuji, its mystical triangle against fluffy clouds ("too symmetrical"), the sterile hotel restaurant ("too empty"); a Tokyo subway ("too crowded"); and dozens of pictures from Philadelphia, but postmarked Tokyo. My favorite was a picture of General George Washington in full military regalia, with Francois's wry greeting, "He didn't sleep here." But most said, "Why aren't you with me?"

I tried to think of his absence as a rehearsal for the rest of my life—without him. But that made me miss him more. Francois seemed the only unordinary thing that had happened to me. Everything else, even the sadness, was predictable. Francois was unexpected, like a remote island off the coastline. You see a dark green spot in the distance, maybe hidden by clouds or rainfall, but you don't imagine you'd go there. But there you are, and it's lovely. Even if you can't stay, you are happy as long as you're there.

I had opened the Beaujolais by the time Francois came up the stairs in late afternoon—I'd bought fresh flowers, too. I stood at the top of the stairs. As he was climbing, he looked up and said, "You look like a breath of spring."

Only French men get away with such corny lines.

When he reached me, he leaned against me and held me a long time before he kissed me. Then he rested his chin against the top of my head. "Why are you so short today?" he asked, confused by my non-tallness.

"I'm wearing flip flops," I explained. "This is my real height."

"You're small," he said with one of his blissful smiles.

"Medium," I corrected him. "Average height for an American woman."

"The perfect height," he said and kissed me again.

Of course, he had brought me a present—a blue kimono, blue as the sky, with deep crimson poppies and swirling white clouds. He draped it over my T-shirt and belted it and then he wound his arms around my waist until his hands found mine. I imagined his arms as a circle that had no beginning and no end.

"I love it," I said. "I'll wear it every morning and…think of you."

At first, I had minded the mornings alone. But after so many of them, I had grown used to waking up to an empty pillow beside me, where Francois ought to be.

"Doesn't Tatiana expect you home tonight?" I asked.

Tatiana had a carousel of romances with filmmakers, writers, philosophers, all of which she managed to broadcast loudly. She was like a one-woman soap opera.

"She'll be back the end of September. You can stay with me," he said. "Why are you smiling?"

"If I were your wife, I wouldn't leave you for a month," I said.

"Ah, if you were my wife, I wouldn't let you go," he said, kissing me again.

We were quiet for a while, in a calming way, when no one has to fill space with useless words. I poured some wine and handed the glass to him—and he said, "Thank you."

"You're tired," I said. "You can sleep if you want to. I mean, sleep as in sleep-sleep."

He said, "There's something we should talk about. It's Princeton."

"So, you're going," I said, heart sinking.

Princeton had been courting Francois Morel a long time, in a slow academic minuet of letters, meetings, lunches, and telephone calls. It was not a question of salary—in Francois's case, he carried an endowment with him, and a counteroffer from the University was a given. But he wanted to expand his research empire. Francois wore his ambition lightly, but that didn't make it any less real.

"Nothing's written in stone, but we're almost there—a few details about resources and staffing. But by next year…"

"By next year, I might be…who knows where," I said, thinking of New York. "Our being apart was inevitable. I hate to think about it, but it's true."

"I don't want that," he said.

"I'm assuming that Tatiana's okay with moving to Princeton."

"Yes," he said, avoiding my eyes.

I seemed to be moving backward, receding, but I wasn't going anywhere—I was standing still, motionless. Once, I might have labeled it an anxiety attack, but that was a false term. It was a reality attack, like cold water after an overdose: of course, a man asked his wife about moving to another city. Any husband would, wouldn't he?

"I'll have funding for a large research center—there's an endowment for $100 million. You'd be an ideal candidate. The job's yours for the asking."

"No," I said. "It's out the question, absolutely not."

"You would have everything you need," he said.

"Not everything, Francois," I said. "Not even close."

"Because it's not tenure track?" he asked—and for such a brilliant man, obtusely.

"This is not about tenure or government grants or even prestige. Not everything is. Can you understand that?"

"Of course, not everything, but you've said you're not sure about teaching," Francois said. "A research position might be the ideal answer, and we'd be together."

"I'm not hanging around waiting and hoping like that Susan Hayward movie, what was that, *Backstreet*?" He looked at me blankly. I explained, "That is an old movie from the '60s. It's one of those Hollywood weepies where the wife's always about to commit suicide so the husband can't leave. In case you were wondering, it doesn't end well. The hero dies and the heroine gets stuck with the kids who always hated her."

"A morality tale, very conventional," he said lightly.

"So am I," I said. "I'm American, remember?"

"You look French," he said, which was really missing the point.

"Francois, please," I said. "Think about what you are suggesting. Everyone would say he did her a favor. I'd be an appendage, or worse than that."

"Nonsense," he argued. "There are dozens of academic couples who publish together, who have intertwined research careers." He rattled off the names of several well-known husband-and-wife teams—mostly anthropologists who, in my view, were strange people to begin with, camping out with tribes who probably pitied them.

"We're not married and we're not living among the Yanomamo," I said. "The reality is that you're allowed one spouse, not two. One per man, that's the rule in this country. I believe it's the rule at Princeton, too."

"You're ashamed of me?"

"God no. I'm proud of you. But I'm ashamed of lying."

"It's not your nature," he said in his sober way.

"I used to have a nature, but who knows where that went? I lost track," I said and polished off a glass of Beaujolais, as if to prove the point.

"No, you haven't," he said.

"That's debatable," I said. "Anyway, I had to invent a new boyfriend to keep my parents off track. They were worried about me not dating after Jeremy. I had to manufacture a man, so to speak."

"Who is my rival, if I may ask?"

"You may. I named him Larry Goldberg and he's at NYU in med school. He is Jewish of course, and from a very nice family. He'd hardly want me schlepping to Princeton. He's a good catch, I think."

"I'm not a very good catch," said Francois.

I kissed him. "No, you are not," I said. "Even if you were not my professor, you'd still be married—and being single is a prerequisite for the eligible category."

"You are a good catch," he said, blissfully.

"Exactly what my mother says," I said. "That's why it's a good thing that I met a wonderful guy like Larry Goldberg, although to tell you the truth, my mother is not wild about him."

"What does she have against poor Larry?"

Francois put his hands inside the kimono, until he found what he wanted.

"Funny thing is, she thinks I'm madly in love with my married professor," I said.

# TWENTY SEVEN

Francois hardly knew Jessica Tang, except as Natasha's protégé. He only met with her as a favor to me. He sat behind his desk, and we sat in front of him, so it felt weirdly formal. I was used to sitting closer.

"This went wrong from the get-go," Jessica said. "Sally went out of her way to make herself a nuisance all semester. She and this other debutante type—named Savannah, if you can believe it—sat together, giggling, making stupid jokes. It was like *Mean Girls*, but *Mean Students*. Disruptive, but nothing I could do. For the final, they sat together as always, which shouldn't have mattered since the test is monitored. But when I checked, their essays were identical—they even started with the very same quotation."

"Which one?" I asked. "There are a lot of poetic quotes on herbal tea packages."

"Cogito, ergo sum," Jessica said.

"I guess that's not such a great one for tea," I said.

"Not in Latin," she said.

Francois stared a long time at his pad. He was taking meticulous notes, and he looked troubled.

He spoke uneasily: "Jessica, why didn't you charge these students with cheating? If the essays were so obviously the same?"

"Natasha warned me not to. Seems Sally Ruder's father is a big donor or something. Plus, she said the girls might say, 'We're Tweedledum and Tweedledee, we walk alike, we talk alike,' blah blah. I let the midterms stand as the final course grade. I told them, the finals were…suspicious."

"So how was that resolved?"

"Well, Sally Ruder's midterm was a C. But, well, it's a little more complicated. You see, she got kind of nuts after the midterm grade, so I told her that she could make it up with her final grade. If she got an A, I said I'd forget the midterm."

"All verbal? Nothing in writing?"

"Yeah, a short discussion," Jessica replied. "I just wanted to get rid of her."

"But you might have said something like, 'You can get an A if you do everything right.'"

"I meant if she listened in class, did well on the final, that kind of stuff," Jessica said.

I saw a shadow cross Francois's face, and I knew something was wrong.

Then he said, slowly, "Please forgive me, but the exam questions are supposed to change every year, to prevent fraud. But you used an old exam. Is that true?"

"Yes," Jessica said. "I was lazy." It wasn't her fault that she had fallen into Natasha's pattern of constant sarcasm, but it didn't sound good.

"Where was Natasha in all of this?" said Francois.

Jessica said, "I've taught this section several times, there was no reason to worry."

"I see," he said blandly. He made a few more notes.

"It's never happened before," Jessica said.

"There's a black market for these exams. So, it has happened. It was a foreseeable event," said Francois. He was in one of his hyper-rational moods.

"I meant, it's never happened to me before," said Jessica.

"I need you to think before you answer," he said. "Is that why you didn't charge the students with cheating? Because you knew you were at fault?"

Jessica looked close to tears. She just nodded, unhappily.

I said, "You're being too harsh."

"Maybe I am," he admitted. "Why don't you give us your perspective?"

"Jessica didn't cheat or lie. She reused an old exam. It was a mistake, and if our undergrads were honest, it wouldn't even be a mistake."

"Jessica skimped on some important details and two clever students exploited it. Natasha should have insisted that the entire class be retested. It wasn't a clean exam, and she knew it. We don't know who else got hold of an older exam. But it's too late. We are where we are." He sighed and looked at me despondently.

"Which is where, exactly?" I asked.

It sounded like wherever we were wasn't good.

"A complaint's been filed against Jessica. I don't know the identity of the student because it's sealed," said Francois. "It might not be Sally Ruder, but chances are, given what I've heard, it is Sally."

Jessica hid her head in her hands.

"Jessica is also a student," I said. "What about protecting her? She has an academic career at stake."

"If this doesn't go away, I'm sunk," said Jessica. "No one will ever hire me."

"Let's not get ahead of ourselves. I'm on the Ethics Committee. I received a notice about it from the new University Ombudsman. You'll get a fair hearing. Maybe you'll get off with a sanction."

"Wonderful," I said. "We have ethics committees to protect kids who cheat."

"That's not all they do," Francois said.

Francois didn't need to tell us. We knew what else.

# TWENTY EIGHT

After my small apartment, Francois's townhouse seemed luxurious. His neighborhood, Society Hill, looked like a tourism brochure, self-consciously "historic," with all the charm of reproduction furniture. The area had been refashioned from a slum—rows of earnest replicas of Federalist and Georgian buildings, a few historical markers. But most residents, like Francois and Tatiana, lived in sleek modern townhouses.

I watched Francois make the tea with a strainer and real mint tea, not teabags. He treated the tea-making process with his usual seriousness. He warmed the flowered pink teapot. I thought, "Francois Morel is the first man to make me tea. I worship him."

But then, there was that sweetly feminine teapot and the flowered tablecloth that was pink and gold. Men rarely went for floral patterns, didn't they? And even French men probably drew the line at pale pink. The kitchen was charming in a wifely way, maybe too wifely?

He was talking about Jessica, again.

"Sally's charging that Jessica gave her the older exam," he said.

"Not Jessica Tang, not possible," I said.

"Well, she's broken some rules," he said, mildly.

"And you and I haven't?"

"Which is why I need to stay far away from this. It's precarious enough being on the Ethics Committee."

"Because of me," I said.

"Because of us," he gently corrected me.

"And you have Princeton to think about," I said.

"And you. I am thinking of your career," he reminded me. Then he added "And yes, Princeton—and why shouldn't I? It matters to me. It matters a great deal."

I saw how hard Francois worked. He never took a day off—not a whole day. I didn't mind. We shared ideas as seamlessly, as effortlessly, as we shared everything else; we were writing a paper together. I fit into his work schedule. But when I didn't...?

He poured the tea into a cup and handed it to me with two lumps of sugar, just as I liked. The tea was much too hot, so I blew on it. For some reason, I thought of Sue's Fast Hair mug, with its cartoon blue-eyed baby.

"I know," I said. "But Jessica's my best friend. I don't see how I can stay away."

"This case is beyond you," he said. "Let Jessica get a good lawyer. That's the sensible thing to do."

"I'm the opposite of whatever sensible is. Look where I am. This is not a reasonable place to be, in some other woman's kitchen. I sneak in and out, like a thief, and I don't even care."

"A lovely thief," he said, and kissed the back of my neck.

I returned to drinking from a cup labeled T, in a curvy script.

# TWENTY NINE

My building was locked when I returned, or rather, when Tatiana returned. It had been an idyllic respite with Francois, but it was over. Worse, my building was in chaos.

"I'm upgrading our security," my landlord explained in a state of paranoid ecstasy.

Morgan wasn't all that bad as far as landlords go. He was a trim dapper guy, probably about fifty, who owned a tiny but pricey restaurant. It had, say, twenty seats and ten skinny young chefs—the type of tony place that was perfect for an ex-stockbroker's second career, the one where he lost the fortune earned in the first go-around. And his (very) much younger girlfriend seemed equally ideal—a dancer, with a small head and sleek dark hair, who wore jeans as clingy as tights, and who, oddly, never spoke a word.

I rarely saw them. They floated through dinners out, weekends at the shore, and vacations abroad. When they were home, I tiptoed so as not to disturb their perfect existence—in their white chrome and steel rooms, their dreamy urban lifestyle.

Morgan handed me the new key, "From now on, only you can have the key—no one else, you hear me?"

He had seen Francois going in and out. "I get it," I said.

"The code is going to be 199," he said.

"But that's the address," I pointed out.

"Exactly," said Morgan, and the girlfriend grinned ear to ear.

Well, that was that: I would be forced to buzz Francois in like a guest. First, leaving Society Hill, and now, this—from high to low, in a day.

Self-pity is like any other indulgence: once it starts, it's unstoppable. As icing on the cake, I got a miserable cold and crawled into bed. Francois called, but I was too tired to talk. I didn't want him to see me red-nosed and red-eyed. I lounged in my bathrobe with the latest *Vogue*. I drank chamomile tea. I pored over eccentric photographs of white-lipped women wearing severe black clothes. I thought, I hate all of my colored clothes. If I wore black, life would become better.

I read some of my *Cinderella-in-Reverse* stories, the ones that I had transcribed from the children's interviews. I had asked children to tell me the story first forward, then backward. I laid in bed, surrounded by fairy tales, dreams of pumpkins and princes.

*The Prince and Cinderella get married and everyone in the whole world comes to their wedding in a pumpkin. Their cake is bigger than the moon, so everyone gets as much as they like. The cake is pink and white. It's all lit up with candles, and inside is another perfect cake, and inside that is another, so no one will ever run out of cake, ever. And before, Cinderella had to sweep the room all the time, and her mean sisters yelled at her, and she was crying all the time, because she wanted to go to the ball. She knows she'll meet the prince at the ball. She can only see him there. She can't find him anywhere else. She keeps looking, but he's hiding.*

Eventually, though, I had to eat—one cannot subsist, nutritionally, on fashion magazines. I slogged my way over to the yuppie food emporium, feeling woozy and grumpy—and looking dreadful.

The market was one of those places that acted like a farm. You had to carry your food around in large straw baskets, so you could forget that the strawberries cost more than a sweater. I found myself next to a woman wearing a sleek black dress and kind of cape with a black satin headband. My life being my life: it was Francois's ever-chic wife, standing alongside an equally elegant older woman who had donned a suit, black of course. They stood alluringly, dark fashion icons, irrepressibly European.

"Bella, I was just mentioning you," she said. "And here you are…shopping."

"Yes," I said lamely. I felt as if I should be doing more exciting and ennobling things, like rock climbing or power yoga. I quickly placed eggs and bread in my basket, just to prove the point that I was, indeed, shopping.

"We need tomatoes," demanded the older women in thickly accented English. She had a cloudy gaze and was a few inches taller than elfin Tatiana.

"The one person who's allowed to boss me," Tatiana said, "my mother, of course. Olga Biro, meet Bella Hirsch." She plopped two huge tomatoes in her basket in a bored, distracted way, although I noticed that she had unearthed the two ripest without effort.

I greeted her in a funereal voice. How was it possible that this woman had a mother? I was about to speak French, but my brain became a colander though which all foreign words flowed. A few sped past me: *au revoir, bonjour, merci, enchantée, à bientôt!*

"My mother has taught Byzantine history," I heard Tatiana saying, perhaps as a response to a jar of Greek honey. "She's an expert on the Sack of Constantinople."

It seemed a violent subject for such a mild-looking woman. "Hmm," I said, trying to recall the century of the sack—or was it a siege? Was it the Crusaders or the Turks? It was not an auspicious time to ask, all things considered, although I was curious.

"Not everything," warned her mother, darkly. "It is a vast subject. I certainly do not know everything."

"More than I do," I said cheerfully, and truthfully.

"Well, an American education," she replied as if that said it all. I smiled, since my thimbleful of knowledge about history wasn't much to boast about.

Tatiana said, "My mother thinks Americans know nothing at all, like children. We are trying to tell her that Americans are not as stupid as all that. There are some clever people here. You're an American for instance."

"Yes," I said, again truthfully.

"It is wonderful having my mother here. We're hoping that she'll stay for a few months." She hugged her mother, in case I was not convinced of her daughterly sentiment.

I managed to eke out a smile.

Francois had mentioned a visit, but I had thought that it would occur in a distant future, in some other country where mothers-in-law belonged. And here she was: a scholarly woman who knew of the Emperor Justinian and the Fall of Constantinople. I pictured the three of them, sipping a young wine, discussing the pros and cons of Byzantium. Francois undoubtedly was a dutiful, attentive son-in-law with his penchant for gift buying, and his unfailing courtesy. He was any mother's dream.

"You are the student of Francois, no?" asked the mother, peering at me with faint contempt.

I wished that I, too, were wearing black rather than my faded long denim skirt, which had seen better days. As far as mistresses went, I was not the poster child.

"Yes, this is Bella," said Tatiana, with one of her cat's smiles. "She was helping Francois out…while I was away. You know how men are."

I busily grabbed assorted cans and jars—hearts of palm, artichoke hearts, diced tomatoes, tuna in olive oil, chutney, mustard. Anything to avoid facing the two of them.

"Men are hopeless," opined Mrs. Biro. I wondered if the former (or so I assumed) Mr. Biro had been hopeless. Perhaps his knowledge of Byzantium fell short of the mark, and she had never forgiven him.

Tatiana sighed in agreement. She turned to me. "Francois tells me there's been some unpleasantness about one of Natasha's students? It's quite time-consuming for him."

"Oh, that's why you were mentioning me," I said. "This mess with Sally Ruder and Jessica is on everyone's mind."

"I suppose," said Tatiana in a bored flat voice. "That's not why I mentioned you."

"Oh," I said.

"I mentioned you because of your friend Drew. We were talking about her."

I must have blinked or just looked stunned.

"She is a friend of yours, isn't she?" Tatiana seemed to enjoy watching me squirm.

"If marrying my ex-boyfriend counts, yes," I replied. "But if not, then no, I wouldn't call her a friend."

"Yes, yes, she is marrying Jeremy," Tatiana said, as if this were a trivial point of no concern to anyone who counted. "But what's she like?"

"I don't know. She's talented, she's beautiful," I said, "and she's tall."

"She is tall?" interrupted the mother, understandably lost.

"Well, yes, she is a very tall person," I explained, as if height were an abstruse concept—which for the tiny Tatiana, it might be. "She likes the Yankees, too."

Tatiana explained to her mother slowly and deliberately, "The Yankees are a sports team, Mama. They play baseball in New York City."

"I have heard of the Yankees," said Mrs. Biro gravely. "*Damn Yankees*. I know this."

"Can you trust her? I mean, Drew?" Tatiana asked, looking at me intently.

I have had many bizarre discussions in my time. In my college years, we spent hours deliberating about the sound of one hand clapping, the wisdom of polygamy, how aliens came from outer space to build the pyramids, and if LBJ shot JFK—or was it Castro? But few matched this particular chat for sheer weirdness. I had feared a tense irate grilling about Francois, who was, after all, Tatiana's husband. It was a wife's privilege to be nosy about her husband. Instead, she was probing me about, of all women, Jeremy's girlfriend.

Then it hit me like a long hard slap. I was no threat to Tatiana's marriage. I never had been.

"No, I guess I don't really trust Drew," I said.

"What is trust?" shrugged Mrs. Biro, in the fatalistic way of Eastern Europe.

Tatiana gave me a sharp look and asked, "Sky? What does he say about her?"

"Sky," I repeated. It had been a long time, I thought, since Tatiana and Sky had ended their affair.

"Don't look shocked, Bella. Men and women can stay friends, can't they?" said Tatiana, impatiently. "I know Sky talks to you."

I said, "Sky says that Drew Hayworth is very sexy."

I hated myself for saying it, even though it was the truth—it was catty. But Tatiana had pushed me overboard—deliberately, I thought. I watched her mouth form a hard line and I felt her rage leaking all over the floor, forming a puddle around her. Maybe certain men and women could be friends after they were lovers, but not Tatiana.

"So that's why he got rid of Jeremy," she said.

# THIRTY

After a month of eating, and reading, and living together, my stolen interludes with Francois Morel felt odd. Was it my imagination or had my tables and chairs shrunk? His frame dwarfed my tiny loveseat, and, I saw, he leaned forward in it, ever so slightly, uncomfortable. Had he ever enjoyed sitting in it, that is, when we weren't touching? After seeing Francois enjoying the comforts of a real home, he looked…misplaced. My apartment was hardly a home away from home—but Francois had a perfectly lovely home. He didn't need another.

Besides, his mother-in-law was taking more and more of his time, which meant I saw him less and less. The woman was a spoiler. If I'd had the cash, I would have paid her fare to Europe or wherever, perhaps to visit a famed Byzantine site, where she could pursue her studies in peace, far away.

"Olga is helpful," he said, casually lapsing into first names. "We have a lot of things to do before we move, and that's all in Tatiana's hands. Olga keeps her company. I'm much too busy for that, with the new book, and the grant. Moving is complicated, a lot of tedious details."

He gave me one of his worldly smiles, assuring me that I was anything but tedious. I knew that I wasn't. I was his fun, his escape—a vacation, an ascent in the cloud-covered hills. But a vacation isn't a life. I wanted to be his real life, the one with bills and housecleaning and insurance and whatever else real life was, not that I knew about it or even if I'd be any good at it. But I wanted a chance at it—with him.

"I guess moving is tough," I said. "I wouldn't know."

He caught my meaning. "Bella, the door is open for you at Princeton. It's waiting, if and when you want it. Money's not a problem. I want you there."

"I can't take a job that's given as a favor. That's not a door, it's a trap. I don't want to be your student or your employee, I want to be your equal."

"I'd be more than happy to work for you," he said, kissing me again.

Then we walked downstairs together, so I could push the security code and let him out. No goodbye kiss. We had to part like friends, nothing more. He smiled at me ironically, as if to say, "Isn't all of this absurd?"

It was still early in the afternoon. I felt like a stroll. My few weeks in Society Hill had given me a new sense of Philadelphia—narrow cobbled streets, forgotten rare book clubs, old white churches, tiny cafés with names like Miss Pettigrew's. I lived not far from Delancey Street, with its elegant brownstones, and the sense of another time.

I hadn't gone far when someone tapped me on my shoulder. I spun around to see a skinny fair-haired male, sporting dark Ray-Bans and a flamboyant fedora. It was Peter, the student with the flair for wreaking havoc with my lectures. He stared at me with the manic glint common to all lunatics and conspiracy theorists.

He laughed rather darkly. "I am following you, believe it or not."

"Actually, I do," I said. "What can I do for you?"

"It's about the Jessica Tang case," he said in a voice that might later warn NPR listeners about the vanishing raccoons of Montana, or why goat's milk isn't all that safe.

I stopped him. "How do you know?"

"This is insider stuff," he said, glancing around furtively.

"Peter, you shouldn't be spreading rumors," I said, trying to control my temper.

"*The Gazette* is reporting on this. But I've got my own angle, believe me."

"What angle could you have?"

He whispered, "Confidentially, I've been buying exams from Sally Ruder."

That night, it rained for hours and hours—a thick, cold Pennsylvania rain. I was listening to *Tales of Hoffman*, settling in for a long night's work, when the phone rang. I knew it was Francois. He wanted me to know how much he missed me. I listened and wondered how much time he had.

He said, "What are you thinking?"

I was thinking of Tatiana's smug expression, of her mother's contempt, of how lonely I was.

"I can't get over the fact that you have a real mother-in-law. I can't explain why, but a mother-in-law seems worse than a wife. I can't get my mind around the concept of you and your mother-in-law, of all of you, eating and sleeping in the same house. You're all together and I'm here by myself."

"That has nothing to do with you," he said.

"That's what's wrong, Francois. It's your life and I'm not part of it. It has nothing to do with me. Don't you see? It's not your problem, but it is my problem."

"You sound like you're crying," he said. "Are you?"

I couldn't answer—because I was.

"There's something you want to tell me, isn't there?"

"I'm going to see the Dean about Jessica," I said. "And I know you don't want me to."

"You're treading on thin ice, Bella. Very thin. This situation is delicate."

"But I feel like my whole life's on thin ice. Like I'm slipping around, and I'm going to fall down any moment."

There was a silence, and then he said softly, "I wish I could help."

"You could fix this, you just don't want to," I said in a sharp voice. I had never spoken that way to Francois. I had never considered speaking like that.

And then I slammed the receiver down, childishly, angrily. It happened before I knew what I had done, and I thought he'd call me back. I stayed up half the night, waiting for his call, and then it was light.

# THIRTY ONE

During my much-needed winter break, I ended up cat-sitting for George, the Lowenstein's sweet-tempered orange tabby. My only instruction, aside from feeding him, was to pet George first thing in the morning, because, Mrs. Lowenstein explained, "He gets lonely otherwise." I knew the feeling all too well.

The apartment looked luxurious to my eyes—leather-bound books, a gleaming baby grand piano facing Central Park, a Diebenkorn landscape, an Ansel Adams photograph that looked like an original plate, ornate Persian miniatures with delicate horses. What a relief that George was an ordinary cat, not a rare breed with a squashed face and stubby tail. Warm cat in lap, I worked mornings in a window-lined sunlit room—and I looked down at the dog-walkers, the joggers, the hurried New Yorkers.

Around the third day of my visit, Sky popped up—and after paying his respects to George, said, "You look terrible."

"Migraine," I said, although crying half the night hadn't helped.

"We need to talk. And don't get angry," he said. He poked his head in his mother's refrigerator and emerged with a bottle of chilled white wine.

I thought: Sky Lowe doesn't want to hire me. There were dozens, maybe hundreds, of fabulous women who knew Marty and Brian and everyone else in New York and L.A. There were equal numbers of brainy young men who wore cool spectacles and wrote wistful novels in their spare time. No reason to pick me.

"I don't get angry that easily. You need to do what's right for you."

"So you know I took Jeremy off the sequel?" he asked. "Who told you?"

I was so relieved that I almost let it show. "Tatiana," I said, breathing freely.

"I hope you don't blame me," he said.

"Not unless you fired Jeremy because of Drew, which is what Tatiana thinks."

"Women. I don't get it," said Sky, petting George, who appeared to agree.

"We are mysterious creatures," I said. "Is it true?"

"No," he said. "Your man, Jeremy, is a drag. He's moody. He thinks he's smarter than everyone else—which, maybe he is. But who cares? If I hadn't gotten rid of him, he would have quit. He's not interested in movies, Bella."

"You're not after Drew Hayworth?" I asked.

"I can't get what I need from an actress if we're sleeping together. She wouldn't try to please me on the set—she'd figure she already had me. I need her to be insecure, on edge. I want Drew Hayworth to seduce me onscreen, not off. You have to mold your material, actor by actor, and I taking acting seriously."

Sky was a strange man—one moment, clueless, and the next, sharp as a tack.

He went on, "Anyway, I'm still not over Tatiana, as long we're getting personal."

Sky and I rarely got personal.

"It's hard to get over people, Sky," I said, with a sad smile. "Maybe she isn't over you, either."

"Forget that. If I weren't in film, Tatiana wouldn't look at me twice. Occupational hazard. You're going to have get used to that."

"Get used to what?"

Sky dumped a script on the table. "Movies, power. All of it."

# THIRTY TWO

In horror movies, the house is pitch-black when you return. It's the total darkness that scares you. But there is another kind of fright, when you walk into a room and the radio is on, there is loud music playing but no one leaps out to scream, "It's a surprise!" That is how my building seemed in midday: bright as a chandelier, even though it was a sunny day. Our lights were on timers. The thermostat was controlled.

The brightness felt wrong.

I pushed the door, slowly. It was slightly ajar. Morgan's alarm system was turned off. I found a yellow Post-it Note attached to the panel where I would have punched in the pointless code. "You are safe!" said the note. Safe from what, I wondered?

I headed upstairs, suitcase in hand, each step feeling like a ledge.

My door, or what was left of it, had been ripped apart, with ragged edges sticking out. The white glass doorknob dangled. I slowly, very slowly, pushed the ragged door open.

There sat two very large policemen, whose collective bulk sank my puny, soft Pottery Barn sleeper sofa, threatening to topple it over. I hung up my coat.

"I just got off the train from New York, so fill me in," I said.

"So you're not the woman who called us?" one of them asked. "You didn't ask us to come over."

"No," I said, searching for the Motrin in my handbag. Three ought to do it.

My apartment reeked of stale cigarettes and beer. I saw a lipstick-stained, half-lit stub on one of my flowered plates and an empty bottle of Heineken. This gang hadn't been in a hurry. They had relaxed, had a beer and a smoke.

I grabbed the plate, dumped it in the trash. Then I scrubbed my hands with detergent and scalding water until they burned. I opened every single window to let in icy air—anything to get the smell out.

"Anyone can break a window pane with an ax," explained the younger of the two. "These security systems are a joke."

"Everyone thinks about handguns, rifles, knives—the urban basics," I reflected. "An ax is kind of off-the-charts. But you can find them at any hardware store. They're cheaper than a rifle, and you don't need a permit."

"Yeah," he said, glancing nervously at me.

"When you think about it, an ax is very efficient. I'm surprised they're not more popular," I said. "Probably they're more for rural areas, like chainsaws."

"Your regular thief doesn't use an ax," he said.

The men hauled their forms around the room. I guess that they were checking to make sure that I wasn't hiding a collection of axes or other rural weaponry.

I checked my jewelry box. I didn't have many good pieces, but I had a few: a ring from my Russian grandmother, a locket with sapphires, a Victorian cameo that I'd gotten for my Sweet Sixteen, and a heart-shaped pendant. Ditto, my closet. Nothing was gone.

After that, there was not much to say, except thanks. I walked them downstairs, so I could collect my mail. I heard a loud, awful crunch under my feet.

I knew at once what it was. The one thing I hadn't checked upstairs.

I'd kept my interview microcassettes in a shoebox, part of my self-consciously low-tech profile, along with file cards and legal pads. I had left it out in the open because, really, who steals tapes? TV sets, jewelry, cash, maybe, clothing, but cassettes?

Making backups had been one among many items on my "to do" list. But I had copied a few, forgotten others, and I couldn't recall which was which. It seemed like a clerical detail. I would get around to it. I had transcriptions, but, as everyone knew, invented data were par for the course. Challenges were part of academic jousting, the nastiness right beneath the scholarly veneer. You needed proof, and I'd lost it—my fault, no one else's.

I wanted, desperately, to call Francois, to hear the sound of his voice. But I knew he'd come rushing over, and then, I'd be back to square one, in deeper than ever.

So I curled up in bed and read my favorite interview, the one whose tape had been crushed. I'd read it hundreds of times, but it always made me cry:

*The prince puts a silver shoe on Cinderella and they get married. Before then, Cinderella danced and lost her silver shoe. Before, she rode in a beautiful pumpkin, and before, she was hungry and cold. Her sisters hated her. Her sisters were mean. And in the beginning, she had her own mommy and daddy and her own house. She wasn't called Cinderella then. I don't know what she was called. She had a different name. That was her real name.*

# THIRTY THREE

"The Pierre," my mother noted with disgust as she looked at the cream-colored invitation. How she found it underneath a tall stack of journals was beyond me, but she had her own radar. "What kind of person is Jeremy marrying in the Pierre, which is going to cost a fortune?"

"An actress. She used to be a waitress on the Upper West Side when we first met her," I answered, trying to ignore the fact that my head was splitting, and my apartment smelled like the morning after a bad party. The acrid odor of stale cigarettes and flat beer hung in the air. Even my mother's Chanel No. 5 didn't drown it out. I loathed the smell of cigarettes. I'd never smoked, even as a teen when it was cool, not that I'd ever skimmed the elusive edges of coolness.

"A waitress?" she asked, aghast. "Jeremy is marrying a waitress?"

"Not a real honest-to-goodness waitress, one of those gorgeous actress-slash-waitresses in Manhattan," I said. "She's the star of *Scared Jim*."

"*Scared Jim*? The guys at work say it might get an Oscar," said my father. "Jeremy wrote that, right? Good for him."

At the mention of *Scared Jim*, my mother looked hostile, as she invariably did when she collided with the ever-present popular culture, like Disneyland or McDonald's or TV game shows. "That's not real writing," she sniffed.

"It's called screenwriting," I explained, ignoring her elitist sniff. "*Scared Jim* might win an Oscar. It's a great film."

"What kind of great film? It's for morons with everyone shooting everyone."

"Anyway, I'd be happy about Jeremy's wedding if I hadn't had my door broken down with an ax—and oh, yes, had my data stolen. Except for that trivial stuff, I'd be ecstatic. Seriously, I'd be thrilled."

"That is a most peculiar thing to say," my mother said.

My mother's most recent style aspired to, but did not achieve, the bohemian. Her outfit that afternoon consisted of black opera-length gloves, Bakelite bangles galore, and a flimsy shapeless garment that might have passed for a nightgown; and the thought crossed my mind that it was, in fact, a nightgown.

I shot her a practiced blank stare. "You have a highly peculiar daughter. You must learn to accept this."

"No one is calling you anything," she said. "I hope you're not planning to go to some reception at the Pierre, although the food might be very nice."

I imagined platters of bacon-wrapped shrimp dancing across her imagination, like a culinary version of *The Nutcracker*. My parents judged weddings by the quality of the caterer. The Pierre probably was up there, food-wise.

"Mom, for your information, while I might be peculiar, I'm not insane. I have zero desire to watch Drew and Jeremy march down the aisle. This invitation is a courtesy. No one expects me to attend."

It was hard to untangle my feelings. I felt sad because Jeremy and I were strangers. I felt sad not being in love with him. I felt sad that we weren't friends—but we never had been friends in the first place. All those crazy intense feelings hadn't led us anywhere except to other people.

The conversation got back on track—to the mechanics of breaking into a brownstone with a high-tech security system—who did what to whom and why—and the futility of trying to find worthless tapes which, by now, were in some dumpster.

But the longer we talked, the worse my head throbbed, which gave me new insights. "Everyone says talking makes you feel better, but I think there's a negative correlation between talking and mood. If we keep on going, I'll jump out the window," I observed.

"Your teachers will understand. Things like this happen," advised my mother. She suffered, I guess, from the delusion that your everyday hardworking thief goes after dissertation data.

"Mom, ex-boyfriends getting married is typical. Getting your dissertation data stolen? I don't think so."

"You were lucky," she replied, grabbing a handful of Wheat Thins to calm her nerves. "Suppose you got your throat slashed. Then what would they say?"

"I'd be dead, so it wouldn't matter," I said. "Besides, I wasn't in danger. I wasn't even here, and Sally Ruder's not a killer."

"Who knows?" my mother said.

I handed her the box of Wheat Thins, exhausted.

My father had drifted over to my new door, which Morgan had diligently replaced. Hammers, screwdrivers, every modern miracle thrilled my dad—and to his delight, the replacement door functioned in a door-like manner. He swung it open for another reliability check. We heard loud footsteps, and my father peered down the stairwell. "Honey, someone is coming to see you? Were you expecting anyone?"

I heard a familiar happy voice, clear as a bell. "Dwayne is at your service here."

I ran out to greet him. Dwayne looked nothing if not natty: a sunshine-yellow tie, striped business shirt; leather briefcase, monogrammed with a huge gold D. He fussily inspected the door, as though he had installed it himself.

"Dwayne, not that I'm not thrilled to see you—but I have to ask, why are you inspecting my new door?"

"I see why you're asking. It's a legitimate question. Dwayne has an answer."

"Which is?" I asked.

"Dwayne's moved into other businesses, more related to the selling of insurance. Name it—home, life, health, business, auto— every type of insurance and all at a highly competitive price. This door, it's what we call an insurance event—Dwayne's on it, because Dwayne provided homeowner's insurance for this very building. Dwayne says, you can never be too careful."

"Dwayne has a lot of sense," my mother said.

"And Dwayne offers competitive rates for auto insurance— happy to give a quote to a good friend," he said.

"I don't drive much, because I don't own a car," I confessed.

"Weren't you supposed to move to L.A. and drive out there? Isn't that why Dwayne gave you lessons?"

"Yes, but it turned that I didn't want to—move, that is. So, I didn't need the car, what with not moving to Los Angeles and everything."

Dwayne chortled with his usual glee. "You dumped the guy? Or he wasn't the marrying type of guy?"

"Oh, he is the marrying kind, only not to me," I said, ignoring my mother's hawk-like eyes. "Anyway, I met a new man and we're very happy."

"Love, I get it," he said. "Dwayne's a romantic guy."

"What kind of love? First, you're with someone and then you're not," my mother said, despairingly. She returned to the Wheat Thins for consolation.

"There wouldn't be a lot of movies and books if everyone stayed together. That's how Dwayne sees it."

"Very smart," said my mother, downing a few more crackers. "These are delicious. Does Dwayne want any?" She held out the half-empty box for him, which he graciously refused.

He asked, "So where's the new guy? Why isn't he around?"

I was quick on my feet. "Well, he's a resident at NYU, and he's got these terrible emergencies, like heart transplants. Actually, he has a patient who's very sick right now. It's touch and go, she's…rejecting her transplant."

I had grabbed that plot from a top-rated TV show, where impossibly sexy residents had torrid affairs, mostly with other sexy residents, but sometimes with even sexier patients, not that it did the patients any good. From what I surmised, all of the sexy patients died on the operating table. The sexy residents had a bad habit of leaving screws in stomachs or putting livers instead of hearts into people.

"How did you meet this medical guy, you being in Philly and he being in New York? You sick or something?"

My father laughed heartily, as he always did when there was nothing to laugh about.

"No," I said, struggling to recall which romantic fiction I'd concocted for my parents. Then a light bulb went off, or I thought it did. "My friend Jessica Tang introduced us," I said in a loud assertive voice.

"I thought Sue introduced you," my mother replied, matching my volume.

"Right," I said, with fading confidence. "We met at Sue's before Jessica Tang introduced us again. That's kind of a coincidence, now that I think about it."

"Everyone knows Larry," my mother said. "He's a popular man."

My father offered another wistful chuckle.

"Dwayne gets it," Dwayne said slyly.

"He does?" I asked, astonished.

"The personals—girls don't like to say they do ads, but they do, right?"

I nodded in the affirmative, and so did Dwayne.

"Exactly right," he said. "Dwayne's cousin, Shirley, she met her new boyfriend through the personals. They're Leos, which is a major sign of the Zodiac. A very strong powerful sign, the Lion. Is this Larry a Leo?"

"I don't think so," I said. "But I'm not a Leo."

"Oh, you advertised like, 'Single white female seeking doctor.' It's handy to have a doctor husband in case there's illness. It's like your personal insurance."

"It is handy," I agreed, picturing my future soulmate with a stethoscope and a thermometer, pressing my tongue down to check for those tiny white spots—or were they red? Not that I'd had that many opportunities to hobnob with doctors. I rarely got a cold, and I avoided doctors like the plague. Probably sickly women were better matches for a medically-minded man.

After Dwayne left, my parents regarded me curiously.

"Honey," said my father in a gentle soft voice, "We're worried." He hadn't looked that way since we lost a puppy.

"Dad, this might be a sign, one of those cosmic signals that I'm on the wrong path. I've been weighing other…opportunities."

"What opportunities?" my mother asked, eyes narrowing.

"Movies. I'd develop scripts and find projects. I wouldn't have to move to L.A. or drive anywhere. The job's in New York. I could take the subway or the bus or even a taxi."

"New York," said my mother, as if losing strength by the minute. "Now you want to move back to New York. Because this Larry person is there?"

"Larry Goldberg," said my father, giving me the once-over, and not too fondly.

"Larry has nothing to do it," I said, which was true enough, given this particular Larry's non-existence.

My father said, "That's what we want to talk about."

"No reason to talk about him," I said cheerfully. There was indeed nothing to say.

"I think there is." He looked fearful.

"I'll be honest," I said, abusing that particular word. "I didn't want to say anything in front of Dwayne, but truth is, Larry and I are drifting apart. I think he's in love with his patient, the one with the transplant. I hope she lives of course. She's had a hard life. She's a refugee."

The refugee came from another highly rated TV show about a law firm in which impossibly sexy lawyers had torrid affairs with other sexy lawyers, but sometimes with even sexier clients, all of whom, save the beautiful refugee girl, were guilty as sin. It seemed no innocent person ever strolled into that law firm—none except the pure-hearted refugee girl, who died in any event, although not from a transplant.

My father coughed, and my mother grabbed more crackers—there were one or two left, or maybe just some broken pieces.

Then she said, "Marilyn's son is at NYU. He's a resident there. You remember, Jerry?"

The Jerry in question was a sweet roly-poly boy, one of my childhood playmates. We had collected glistening rocks together.

"Marilyn must be very proud," I said.

"Yes, she wanted Jerry to become a doctor, like his father is—and, I think, maybe his grandfather. So, I said, 'That's wonderful, because Bella's dating someone in cardiology, too, and his name is Larry Goldberg.' And she said, 'I'll ask Jerry if he knows this Larry person, because why shouldn't he?'"

I nodded uneasily—the conversation was heading downhill, and fast.

"Well, Jerry didn't know him, because there is no Larry Goldberg who is a resident at NYU. I said, 'That must be impossible,' and Marilyn said, 'No, there is nobody with that name.' Can you imagine?"

"Huh, not even one," I mused.

"No, not even," said my mother. "There's not even a person named Goldberg."

"You'd figure there'd be at least one Goldberg in a medical school. What are the chances?" I fake-laughed, hoping to encourage my father to join in the general mirth, but he looked stony-faced. I felt like taking a nap—that's how bored I was with Larry and everything else.

"Something is the matter with you," my mother almost whispered.

Of course, something was the matter. But it wasn't one single thing that was easy to repair, like a leaky roof. Many things were the matter, starting with Francois Morel, and maybe ending there, although having my data stolen was no help. Plus, there was Jessica Tang's hearing looming, and yes, the mess of having lied to everyone—and badly. Anywhere my mind wandered, something was out of order.

I said, "Well, it's like this. The thing about Larry Goldberg is that there never was a Larry as in one single boyfriend. There was never an actual person in the strict sense of the word 'actual.' He was what you call an amalgamation, a prototype of, you know, different men that I'd dated from time to time, here and there."

My parents stared and then coughed.

My father asked, "So you were dating lots of different doctors?"

"Not exactly medical doctors," I answered him, as if weighing a philosophical question. "Perhaps, more like a PhD kind of a doctor."

"Oh," he said.

"Still, a doctor, right?"

"Oh," he said again and coughed.

It wasn't my most polished performance, but it beat telling the truth about Francois and me. Everyone on talk shows raves about how honesty is the best policy, but it's not all that great as a family communication strategy.

My mind-reading mother said, "You are the world's worst liar."

"It's never actually been a goal of mine," I replied.

"Ha ha," laughed my father melancholically.

"But I'm not lying about the job in New York," I said.

"But there's your PhD," said my father.

"Was," I corrected him. "There was my PhD."

My father continued: "You left Jeremy and New York because you were so sure about a PhD. You said, 'Dad, I am one hundred percent sure.' Those were your exact words."

"So?" I asked. "I changed my mind about what I'm sure about."

"Maybe you should talk to someone," my mother suggested.

"Actually, I am talking to someone," I replied. "I am talking to my parents."

She sagged. "I mean, to a professional—and don't look at me that way."

If she had her way, half the world's adult population would be on some psychiatrist's couch, sobbing their hearts out and ranting about their tortured childhoods.

"First of all, I don't think talking is helpful whether I pay for it or it's free. Talking is not all it's cracked up to be, and personally, I don't see why everyone is doing it all the time. And second of all, I don't need therapy just because I invented a quasi-boyfriend who's in medical school, which I'm sure lots of women do—maybe not lots, but some."

"Bella, in two years, you'll be thirty…" my father began.

"Twenty months, but who's counting? But whether I'm teaching or not, chances are that I turn thirty. Aging is what happens unless it's interrupted, say, by getting your throat slashed or you die in a car crash or you get a rare tropical disease, in which case, you don't turn thirty. But that is totally independent of the career thing—unless you choose a high-risk career, like being a stuntwoman. Obviously if I become a stuntwoman, I might not turn thirty or even twenty-nine."

My father looked stunned. "Don't be morbid," he said.

I gave him a hug and then rested my head on his shoulder. "Don't worry. I am really not a lunatic."

"Lunatic, ha ha," said my father sorrowfully.

Out of left field, my mother said, "What does your professor say about this?"

"I haven't talked to Natasha Lowenstein yet."

My mother shot me one of her "who-are-you-kidding" looks. "I didn't mean Natasha," she said, patiently. "I meant, your French professor."

"Francois Morel," I said. My voice had somehow cracked. "He's going to Princeton next year. It doesn't matter."

She looked down and murmured, "Oh."

# THIRTY FOUR

From *The Daily Pennsylvanian*:

Daniel and Lilith Ruder Donate $25 Million to Establish New Theater Complex at the University

*Beverly Hills real estate executive and University Alumnus Daniel Ruder and his wife, Lilith, have donated $25 million for a state-of-the-art multi-media performance and exhibition center. Plans for the new Center, to be called The Ruder Center for Community and the Arts, were announced yesterday. Mr. Ruder, recently elected to the Board of the University, called it a "special honor" to be able to contribute to the school that now serves the second generation of his family—his daughter, Sally Ruder, currently is a junior majoring in political science.*

*"Lilith and I are humbled to have our name linked to a school that has given our family so much," said Mr. Ruder.*

Jessica flung the campus paper on the floor and spent a few minutes spewing ugly profanities and kicking desks and chairs. She hurled a ball of paper across the room, which sailed past my head, missing it by a small margin. Then she kicked a few more objects.

"Jess, you won. It's over," I said. "Relax, okay?"

"Won what? All my friends from college are making tons of money, or more money than I'm going to make in the next zillion years. And I have to fight to keep a lousy graduate stipend, which I can hardly live on, by the way."

We all received the same stipend. It wasn't a great deal by "real world" standards, but it paid the rent and bought groceries. Was it supposed to do more?

"Natasha will handle it," I said. "There's always a way to get around these rules."

"If you're a rich spoiled undergrad, there is. Tell me that the Ruders aren't going to get Sally's grade changed to a B."

"You don't know that," I argued.

"What world are you living in? You think Dan Ruder gave twenty-five million dollars for nothing? Suddenly, he woke up and said, 'Hey man, let's go build a center!' And it happens to be when his crazy daughter's caught cheating? Give me a break. Sally's getting what she wants the way these rich kids always do. The school has been courting Daniel Ruder for years. They always pursue wealthy alumnae. Now they'll go after Sally."

"Oh, that's just gossip."

"Why are you defending Sally? She broke into your apartment and tried to destroy your academic future."

"No, this was more like one of those kooky sorority-fraternity pranks, where they dip someone's head in cow's blood or they make them tango naked. Rich kids' fun. She didn't take jewelry or anything valuable. How could she guess that I didn't have backups? No one would believe it."

"Why didn't you?" Jessica asked.

"I am a wild and reckless person," I said. "Why did you reuse an old exam?"

"You want the truth?" asked Jessica.

"Not me," I said. "I prefer total unadulterated fiction."

"Here it is—the naked truth, take it or leave it. Natasha said that I shouldn't waste my time on teaching. She said teaching was a trap—don't get caught. Just focus on publishing. And guess what? I listened."

I could hear Natasha's light irony, playful and dismissive. She hadn't meant her words to be taken seriously, she never did. Natasha was an excellent teacher.

"I'm sorry," I said.

"She's sorry, you're sorry, everyone is sorry," she shrugged. "I know what you're thinking, that you'd never reuse an exam, no matter who said what. You're too smart for that. You're too ethnical."

"Anybody can do anything, Jessica. Until you do something, you think, oh, I'd never do that. But then it's done, and it turns out that 'never' wasn't real," I said.

"Oh, I'm going to miss you," said Jessica.

"Me too," I said. "But, Jess, why quit? Natasha doesn't want you to leave, does she?"

"I can't face her now," she said. "Besides, I have friends…they're working at a new company. It's growing fast. They're looking for a researcher, and one thing I'm good at is research. They say I can get options if I join, so why not?"

"Options," I said. "Is that the same thing as stock?"

I knew there was something called a stock market that zoomed sky-high, and then plummeted, causing people like my father to lose money at regular intervals like clockwork. Apparently, he bought when times were good and sold when times were bad, while clever people called investors did the opposite. My knowledge of the stock market stopped there. I listened to Jessica's explanation about options and strike prices, most of which flew over my head. Learning the price of eggs had been hard enough.

"You probably don't know university presidents make just as much as most CEOs," she said.

"I never think about money," I said, "If I don't owe anything, I feel rich."

Moments before, I had pitied Jessica like a stray kitten, but that was from the slanted angle of the university, where people battled over footnotes. Jessica would do fine. She would soon be pouring fancy Cabernet at an upscale bistro, chatting about her condo in D.C. or Malibu or wherever people bought condos. No telling what you could buy if you got those options.

"Debt isn't bad. How do you think all those Hollywood movies get made?" asked Jessica, laughing. "Anyway, are you going to finish your *Cinderella* study?"

"Not me," I said. "Another fairy godmother."

# THIRTY FIVE

If it had been a movie, I could have fast-forwarded. A rapid dissolve from Philadelphia and there I'd be in Central Park. One shot, a lovesick student, and the next, clinking champagne glasses at the Oscars. In real life, though, moving from Point A to Point B is agonizingly slow, like finding a parking spot on Saturday night. In movies, the hero just parks, but in the real world, you wander for hours hoping to find a spot.

Francois and I hadn't been alone since the phone call in the rain when I had slammed the receiver. After that, our encounters were strained: He looked sick when he saw me, and I dropped whatever I was carrying. I avoided campus.

I hung around a local "arty" video store, whose staff consisted of a few ironic young guys who would have died and gone to heaven if they'd suspected that I knew the likes of Sky Lowe. I preferred to hang out incognito, so I could spy on who rented what and who said what and report back to Sky. It gave me something to do when I had nothing to do.

All of the so-called clichés turned out to be true: Single youngish women loved tony costume dramas with handsome lords and lovely ladies; single youngish guys wanted sci-fi and big-budget action flicks; and couples split the difference by renting films that, presumably, neither liked. I defied stereotype by watching stacks of 1950s Westerns—stories of tall men taming the wilderness, against open sky and sunlit mountains—films like *The Man from Laramie, Shane, Winchester 73* and *The Searchers.*

"It couldn't kill you to watch something new," one video guy drawled.

"Not if it's romance," I said as the mirthful eyes of Julia Roberts bore down on me from the poster high above the counter.

"I hear you," he said, chuckling sadly.

"But you're right. It's time to mix things up—bring me your favorites."

He and his fellow ironists took my request with unusual seriousness, checking my rental profile and so forth. After a few minutes, they handed me *The Crow, The Mask, Natural Born Killers*, and *Ed Wood*. That night, I dipped into the new film decade, where reality and unreality bled together and came apart.

I called Sky. "*The Crow*. It's gorgeous, the colors are so electric and moody, like adolescence. It's almost poetic."

"The eye gets smarter," said Sky, ever-quotable. "In a few years, there won't be much we can't do—visually, that is. Stories, that's different."

"I think the plots are sort of ho-hum. They lack heart."

"Hey, the heart doesn't get any smarter. We've got to settle for the eyes."

Sky was right: The heart doesn't get smarter—sadder, maybe, but not smarter.

Not thinking about Francois had been my only New Year's Resolution, but I broke it every day, every hour. My pledge had the effect of focusing my mind on Francois as though I'd resolved in quite the opposite direction. Such was the imperfect power of resolution, I reasoned: You can't will yourself to fall in or out of love.

At the month's end, I heard from Francois. "I have something for you," he said, sounding tense. "I'd rather give it to you in person, it's…confidential."

"Very cloak and dagger," I replied, since Francois was the opposite of theatrical.

"Everyone departs from his style once in a while," he said.

I suggested a rather old-fashioned piano bar on a quiet street. The bar was straight out of film noir, with a middle-aged, slick-haired man playing love songs with minor chords, with lyrics like *Melancholy Baby* or *Blue Moon*. It was smoky, not too crowded. At first, I didn't see Francois—he was near the back, where there was even less light, facing the rear wall. He wasn't reading or pretending to do anything aside from waiting for me. We'd both arrived more than a quarter hour early—one of our shared quirks, our fear of lateness. By this time, it didn't matter who saw us together.

I tapped his shoulder, and just seeing his face made me unreasonably happy. He helped me off with my coat, and hung it carefully, gingerly, as if it were mink—rather than a plain down jacket.

An officious young waiter materialized, and coolly rattled off the wine choices. The merlot, I heard, was "friendly and approachable" and two glasses of it (or another equally sociable vintage) arrived shortly. I reflected, not for the first time, that wines were turning friendlier as people became less so.

"It's freezing," I said, shivering in my tissue-thin cashmere sweater, which I'd worn, naturally, out of vanity. Without comment, Francois untied his huge scarf and passed it to me. I tried to ignore the bare space on his neck, which the untied scarf had revealed—and I buried myself in his soft scarf, which smelled like him, too.

"Now you're warm," he said, as proud as if he'd knitted the scarf for me.

"So? What's the secret?" I used the word "secret" in mental quotes, since I had deduced that it was a pretext to see me again.

I was mortified when Francois's head ducked under the table, and he emerged with an old shoebox. On its outside, an index card with my name printed neatly. I lifted the lid, then shut it quickly as if it were Pandora's Box. I tried to mask my disappointment.

"This won't make a difference," I said. I thought I was talking about school, but was I? As hard as it was to know someone else's mind, it was harder to know my own.

"I didn't think it would. But these are yours. You should have them."

Each of my audiocassettes was dated and numbered, held together by neat thick rubber bands and lined up in a shoebox. Francois knew my weakness for paperclips, rubber bands, file cards, erasers, lead pencils, lined paper, all those schoolgirl tools that were fast vanishing. But as orderly as the tapes were, I felt less so—or rather, the order they had didn't correspond to anything in me.

"You've done a good job, and thank you," I said. "Now explain how you got these, if you don't mind."

"When I heard about the break-in, I took a gamble that Sally Ruder kept the tapes—lunatics rarely act as others think they will, which is part of their lunacy. Before the break-in, Sally was a cheater, but now, she was a thief, which she didn't care about. So I called the one person who would—care that is."

"I can't imagine who would," I said.

"Sally's father—Dan Ruder, as you may know, was very intent on serving on the Board of Trustees. I figured out that Sally was selling exams and told him that I wouldn't press charges about it—on two conditions: one, that Sally drop all of her charges, and two, that she return certain audiotapes. He's not a stupid man. So, Sally sent them to him and then he sent them to me—she has no idea I'm involved."

I was amazed. Francois was the last man on Earth to take risks—he was philosophically opposed to them. Life, in his view, was fraught with enough dark sorrows; why invite more? Yet he'd gotten the job done with so little fanfare, and all while we were not speaking.

"You are a natural diplomat. They should send you to the Middle East," I said.

He sipped more wine, pleased at the thought. "Not everything needs a noisy battle and a big drama. Some things need tact."

"It's not fair, you playing the unselfish White Knight and forcing me to admire you all over again," I said.

"I'm extremely selfish, and a middle-aged professor makes a poor sort of White Knight," he laughed.

"Please, you're not even forty," I said, and felt a pang thinking of him growing old without me. I might have contradicted the selfish part, too, if my shyness about sex talk hadn't prevented me. I blushed easily.

"By my age, Mozart was dead," he sighed.

Men of ambition were forever failing by some manly metric: they hadn't made a great fortune, climbed Everest, won the Nobel, written *The Marriage of Figaro*, or discovered a new species of flora or fauna. It required a lazy sort of guy to label himself a success, and Francois was anything but lazy—or boring.

"Don't fall into the Mozart Syndrome. You're not old," I said.

"I feel old. I wish we'd met when I was twenty. I was shy, though, very serious. You might have scared me."

"Hmm, when you were twenty, I was ten, so that would have been scary in a different J.D. Salinger-way, which is kind of unsavory."

"Well, when I was thirty, then—that sounds much safer."

I had a vivid flashback to my twenty-year-old self: quoting stray bits of Rilke to a bleary-eyed, guitar-strumming boyfriend. I'd read long gloomy Russian novels in which it was always winter, and I'd opined that there was little hope for mankind. "I was a…late bloomer," I told him. "I think you met me at the right time, except for the marital status thing."

Perhaps I was still shivering, because Francois signaled the waiter and ordered us a pot of mint tea with "real sugar" for me. I started talking about *The Searchers*, and how I cried at the ending, and how much I loved rereading Trollope's *Barchester Towers*, and how I had rid the world, once and for all, of the young transplant doctor, Larry Goldberg.

"Poor Larry, a life cut short but full of promise," I laughed.

Francois smiled, and said, "I've been so lonely without you, Bella."

"It is lonely," I admitted. "I don't have another friend like you. There's no one I really like as much, not in the whole world."

"I think the proper word is 'love.'" Only Francois would put the words "proper" and "love" together.

The waiter laid out the tea, the sugar cubes, a fragile cup, and a tiny spoon—and I warmed my hands against the chubby pot, which emitted a thin stream of steam. We spent the next hour or so talking of Francois's new book, which was to popularize his experimental research. Francois was an intellectual snob—and he feared, as purists do, that he might cheapen his scientific theorizing. "But at this stage, it's required," he said as he poured the tea.

"Why not reach a broader public, Francois? There's no harm in making money, or is that against your code of honor?"

"You sound like my mother," said Francois, affectionately. He wasn't one of those American men who blame all woes on mama. From him, it was a compliment.

We relaxed for a while—me drinking sweet mint tea, and Francois sipping wine. I felt ridiculously happy, just sitting there talking to him or not talking, enclosed in his soft scarf. It was crazy.

Francois said, in a low voice, "I know you're disappointed. You deserve more."

I don't why, but what I said was: "I don't deserve more than you. I'd be more than fine with you. All you have to do is tell me there's a chance, and I'll wait. No questions, why or how long. I know it's kind of Nineteenth Century, but that's how I feel. Call it faith."

I always wondered what that old musty canard "heart in mouth" meant. Now I knew. I didn't care if I sounded foolish or even foolhardy. Francois had a careful nature; he weighed his actions, one by one. I'd caught him off guard. His eyes met mine, as if taking me in for the first time, as I was, all the old paint stripped away and just me underneath.

He said, "You are something."

I tried to keep my voice steady. "I don't want to be something. I want an ordinary life. I want to be an ordinary person doing ordinary things, but with you."

I imagined his decision matrix, his mental calculations: total hours spent negotiating, dividing assets, explaining to colleagues and family. Divorces were messy and sprawling; they ate up lives and time. It was fine, more than fine, to rush into a lover's arms, and quite another to schedule a tedious lawyer's appointment. I had no idea of whether Francois and Tatiana had property in France or anywhere else. I'd never asked, but then, it wasn't my property to divide.

"You'll never be ordinary," he said. "You could never be."

I've noticed that music and mood often meld—as if some unseen accompanist is listening to our secret thoughts. The pianist's melodies turned wistful and soulful—maybe he played *Georgia on My Mind*. I hid my face in Francois's soft scarf, wishing I could disappear into it, stay there.

He continued: "I have so much going on. The move to Princeton, the research center, a new book. There are too many moving parts in this picture. It wouldn't be fair to you."

"You're talking as if I wanted to live in a cave and wear sackcloth. No one's living on bread and water in New York, unless they're a fashion model, in which case, forget the bread, too."

"Be serious, Bella. This doesn't make any sense—you're young."

"I'm younger than you, but I'm not that young. And it's when life gets serious, that's when I need to laugh. So seriously, what makes sense? That I sleep with other men even though I'm in love with you? Or that we keep having an affair and I keep lying to everyone? Either one doesn't sound so smart to me. They sound pretty grim."

"You can't put your life on hold," he said, "even if you believe you can, you can't."

"My life isn't my sex life—or are you becoming a Freudian?"

"No, and you're twisting my words, which I know you like to do. You're going to be leading a very different life. You'll meet new people."

I could have catalogued Tatiana's highly public infidelities—but that was her business—and Francois was mine, if he wanted to be. I said, "I'm not fickle. Are you?"

"It's not about me. Tatiana left a marriage because of me. It's not her fault that I don't love her, and I love you. I can't blame her for that, or even for the kind of marriage we have. Whatever happens has to be her choice—I owe her that much. I won't make a promise that I can't be sure of honoring, and neither should you."

I exhaled slowly. The sounds of the bar returned. Dinner hour had started. The room was filled with expensive-looking beautiful men and women, faces shining, lit by candles, drinking all that friendly wine. The piano had stopped, too—it wasn't the time for melancholy ballads. Maybe after dinnertime the music would start again, and by then, only the solitary people would be listening.

I suppose that I felt too numb to cry. I had climbed out on a ledge, too far to return. I didn't regret the dare, only the bruises. Francois was lazy about himself. He wasn't the kind of man to turn his life upside down for something like love—and I was just starting to figure out the kind of woman that I was.

He walked me home, shoebox in one arm, me in the other. The sky was black and the streets were deserted. A fierce, bitter wind pushed against us, and he held me tightly. I had forgotten, perhaps by design, to remove his scarf—but when we arrived at my building, I took it off and gently wrapped it around his neck, as many times as I could, and then I let go of him, and he handed me what was mine. Neither of us managed a word. Then he kissed me goodnight, hardly touching me, as though we were both made of glass and might splinter into the night air—and I walked into my building, without him, without looking back.

# THIRTY SIX

Helping Jessica pack was like a trip down Grad Student Memory Lane—the good, the bad, and the ugly. The two of us were yin and yang—I had a habit of throwing out everything, and Jessica was a confirmed packrat.

"Fare thee well, *Syntax of Imperatives*. Adieu, *Probability Theory*," I said as I dumped them into Jessica's boxes, all neatly labeled. "Seriously, will you ever read this stuff again?"

"I might."

"Not I," I said. "If you ever catch me reading these, you'll know I've gone off the deep end, or the deeper end."

"That's you, always so sure," she said.

"But usually wrong," I admitted. "I can't think of much I've been right about. I thought I found Jeremy his dream job, but all I found was his dream wife. And I thought I'd love teaching, and I hate it. And, then, you know…"

"You're thinking about Francois Morel," she said.

I didn't need a reason to think of Francois—I just had to wake up or go to sleep, or not.

"Do you have a type?" I asked her after a while. "A person that's perfect for you?"

"I never thought of it that way," she said.

"Neither did I, or I thought that I didn't. But funny thing is, Francois Morel is my type. His accent, his big sweaters, how serious he is—everything is my type. It's like there is an algorithm and he's what popped up as the solution. I can't accept that he'd stay married to the wicked witch when I know that I am his type. And believe me, I am not every man's dream—not just on the outside, on the inside."

Jessica studied me and said, "You're fooling yourself."

"You mean, about the marriage part," I said.

"No, about you," she said. "Suppose Francois left his wife. And then, he asked you to give up New York and film, and move to, say, Ann Arbor. He said, forget about work, you can hang out, read books, have kids. Would you do it?"

"Too many hypotheticals," I said, lowering my eyes.

"You can deal with them," she said. "We know your answer, right?"

I made an upside-down smile, because yes, we did know.

"Years ago, Francois warned me that research happens at a certain time, in a certain place. I think relationships are the same. If he'd asked me to marry him, I would have in a heartbeat. I would have gone anywhere he asked. But I fell in love with this movie, with having a…career."

"And you got one," she said. "Actually, you earned one."

"Maybe I am a feminist and I didn't know it. That is, if feminists go in for shopping and makeup."

"You can be a closet feminist," she said.

"What about you—if Natasha asked you to give it all up?"

"I do want the whole domestic thing—home, dog, kids. But I'm done chasing. If Natasha wants me, she's got to chase me. Once I'm out of here, well, it's a big world."

"And better dressed," I joked. "I can't wait to be out of here."

"But you seemed so into your *Cinderella* study," she said.

"The kids' stories don't need me. They're perfect just the way they are," I said. "My heart's not in academia the way yours was. You're the real thing, Jessica."

"Don't act like I won't be a serious researcher—I will be. But as far as academia, no, I'd never have the nerve to return."

"We're sounding like *The Wizard of Oz*," I said. "We are the Cowardly Lion and the Tin Man, aren't we?"

"Well, we do have brains. I think that's enough to go anywhere."

"You're going where?" my mother asked in a state of shock.

"The Oscars," I said—*Scared Jim* had received four Academy Award nominations: for Best Director, Best Film, Best Editing, and Best Original Screenplay. "I get to wear that gown, the Grecian-style gown, the one you talked me into."

"I told you you'd need a good dress," she said. We paused to reflect on its diaphanous layers of chiffon, draping to the floor, goddess-like.

"You were right," I admitted.

"I know," she said, annoyed. "You need the right shoes. Nothing too high, though. I'm sure you can find them on sale."

"Sky says I can buy anything I like and charge it to the business on an expense account. I mean, not a house or a car, although some of those gowns that actresses wear cost more than a car," I said.

"Not that they look it," she said. "I worry about you working in movies. These people, they just drink and take drugs, and they're always marrying and divorcing."

"Everyone everywhere drinks and takes drugs and gets married and divorced. You only read about the Hollywood people because they're better looking," I said.

"True," she said unhappily. "No one reads, either."

"Sky Lowe reads Jane Austen. He loves Jane Austen."

"Oh," she said, taken aback at the mention of the divine Jane. "And what does his sister have to say about your leaving?"

"At first, Natasha was miffed, but now, I'd say she's happy."

"Why would she be happy?"

It was time to come clean.

"I returned the tapes to Natasha and the department. They funded me while I worked for Sky, so it's the fair thing to do. My guess is that Natasha will write a book on the stories."

"She wouldn't dare!" my mother exclaimed, horrified. "It's like stealing!"

"Mom, I'll be one of those footnotes, the kind everyone gossips about at those conferences, like, 'You know, that grad student did all the work.' It's right here in the footnote on page 202, just look. So that's a kind of posterity."

"You killed yourself for a lousy footnote," she said, "a footnote."

"And don't forget, a producer's credit," I replied.

# THIRTY SEVEN

Later on, I went to many red-carpet evenings, but I always treasured the first: a limo at the airport whisking me to a large hotel, a mirrored lobby where people called me by my last name, the nervous hotel clerk wishing me good luck and her reverent tone as she handed me Sky's messages about something called a "swag bag," which the clerk translated into "gift bag," so heavy that a porter had to haul it. I had never seen anything remotely like it. I spent a few hours sorting through the stuff: a pile for my parents (a platinum watch, Coach luggage), for Jessica (a gaming console), and Ben and Sue (Tiffany cocktail shakers.) I kept a pair of pearl earrings for myself, as a souvenir.

As I had predicted, *Scared Jim* did win the Academy Award for Best Screenplay. Jeremy accepted with a shy thanks and a loving glance to his wife. But later, Sky Lowe took the podium—a surprise win for Best Picture.

Sky rattled off about a dozen names in ten seconds—and then he slowed down. He said, "Movies happen in strange ways. One rainy night, some student I hardly knew dragged me to her apartment to read some unknown, unpublished stories. She would not take 'no' for an answer, and she never has. So thank you, Bella Hirsch, for being stubborn. You made this one happen." And he held the golden Oscar up above his head, so I could see it.

All that I could hope was that my mother and father were watching and saw me—also that my mascara wasn't going to turn into a big black smear, because I started crying just as the cameras hit me.

We ended up at a party. The big one, all pink and yellow lights and noise. I felt like I'd been parachuted into a camp of famous drunken people—well, some were drunk, others were in rehab. But it turned out that Sky's speech had made me into a mini-celebrity. *Variety, The Hollywood Reporter,* even *Entertainment Tonight* swamped me with questions about *Scared Jim* and Sky. And there was a guy, in a weird plaid suit and an awful tie, who kept on pestering me all night, but that's another story.

And before the night ended, I found Jeremy. By now, he was teaching creative writing at Columbia—so we were about to switch roles, which made perfect sense in a way.

I leaned on him and said, "I never got a chance to thank you. It's because of your writing, it's because I knew you that I'm here. I got everything backward—I kept on thinking that you owed me, and it turns out that I owe you. I'll never be able to thank you, not in a million years, Jeremy."

He smiled and said, "I think you just did."

And I whispered into his ear, "You knew all the time, didn't you?"

"About Francois, yes," he answered. "You're a bad liar, Bella."

"And you don't hate me for lying?"

He tilted my head up to meet his and said, "No, never. You'll always be my first love, there's only one. And we were both lucky."

"Very lucky," I said, and I meant it.


Later, as I was flying home over the wispy, white clouds, I thought about how everything had spun by me, as the Bard says, swift as a shadow and short as a dream. I wished that I could rewind it, and play it over and over, only this time slowly—but then I'd miss what came tomorrow, wouldn't I? And I looked around where other passengers were sitting and reading and eating—and if I thought about it, all of us were all flying together.

In the middle of my reverie, I was prodded by the same pest I'd seen last night at the Oscars party. Last night, he had worn a loud plaid suit with a dark shirt, which, I imagine, was part of a new retro look, or perhaps an evil conspiracy by the fashion industry to make men look silly. Today, in sweats and jeans, he looked harmless enough.

"Hello again, I switched seats," said the guy, as if we were buddies. "Well, to be perfectly honest, I switched my flight from New York, where I live, to Philly, where I don't live. Sky Lowe says you're tough to get between boyfriends, not to get too personal or anything. I didn't want to waste any time, so here I am."

He didn't look like the kind of guy who minded being personal with anyone. But I was sure he was wasting his time—and what was his name?

"I need to work on the flight," I said, in a not-too friendly way.

He wrestled with his seat belt. "Sure thing," he said. "When you're in New York, I could take you to a great comedy club. You like standup, don't you?"

"Oh, that part of my life is over," I sighed.

"Comedy? You don't like comedy?"

"No, dating. Dating is off for now. It has nothing to do with you, obviously. I mean, meeting you didn't *cause* me to stop dating. It's like a Zen Buddhist thing, like monks don't date, do they? Not that I am actually a Buddhist."

Before I finished speaking, he bent over, sorted through a jam-packed briefcase, pulled out a screenplay, opened my airplane table, and plopped the screenplay on it. I stared at it in disbelief and cracked up.

"*Monks on a Mission*? You seriously expect me to read this *now*?"

"Well, they're not really monks, they're CIA agents dressed as monks," he said cheerfully. "You said you wanted to work, didn't you?"

"I guess I did," I said.

"By the way, you don't need any excuses, like you've sworn off dating, Bella."

"I wasn't making excuses, Mr...." I noticed his eyes were a bright blue.

"Larry, please," he said. "Larry Goldberg."

# ABOUT THE AUTHOR

231

Carla Sarett is a poet, essayist and fiction writer based in San Francisco. Her work has appeared in *Thimble, Blue Unicorn, San Pedro River Review, Naugatuck River Review, ONE Art, Hobart Pulp, Across the Margins, Prole* and elsewhere; her essays have been nominated for the Pushcart Prize and Best American Essays. THE LOOKING GLASS, a novella, (Propertius Press) was published in October, 2021. Carla has a Ph.D. from University of Pennsylvania. A CLOSET FEMINIST is her debut novel.

# ABOUT THE PRESS



Unsolicited Press was established in 2012 and is based in Portland, Oregon. The team produces poetry, fiction, and nonfiction by award-winning and emerging writers.

Learn more at www.unsolicitedpress.com.